BODEN'S P
A BRITISH
WASN'T MU

...OUT IT....

The British tanks were closing in, and Boden could sense Seebohn's desperation. He gloomily suspected that Seebohn was re-enacting the events of 1918, and even playing out his father's experiences.

There was another crack above their heads, and this time part of the ceiling of the abandoned house fell in behind them, bringing with it a cloud of dust that mingled with the smoke from the burning timber behind.

Another round from the closing British cruiser brought down the wall beside the window, and exposed the port side of the panzer's hull.

Boden checked the sight and felt for the firing button with his left hand.

When he depressed it there was only an empty click....

Panzer Platoon: Blitzkrieg!

GUNTHER LUTZ

SPHERE BOOKS LIMITED
30/32 Gray's Inn Road, London WC1X 8JL

First published in Great Britain by Sphere Books Ltd 1977

Published by arrangement with the author's agents

TRADE
MARK

Set in Monotype Baskerville

Printed in Great Britain by
Hazell Watson & Viney Ltd
Aylesbury, Bucks

1 5th Moroccan Spahis

When Micki Boden first saw the troop of French Colonial Cavalry charging the Panzer Column he frowned in bewilderment and grasped the reassuring solidity of the Mark 2 panzer turret hatch to prove to himself that he wasn't dreaming.

A Hotchkiss gun maybe, a Renault Char B Medium tank perhaps, but the Colonial Cavalry, that really was a surprise, even though they were a few hundred metres inside the French frontier.

Simultaneously he was overwhelmed by a feeling of relief after the tense hours crossing Luxembourg on the road from Trier; twisting along the overhangs of the Semois River above the deep gorges of the Ardennes. Up to that point there had been no opposition, although they had all advanced without talking, expecting at any moment annihilation from the one hundredweight shells of the 155 mm Schneider batteries, deep in their concrete casemates along the Maginot Line, fifteen miles away.

The Unteroffizier of Number 6 Platoon, 31st Panzer Regiment, blinked and put up his goggles to the edge of his black beret, since, for the moment, there was no dust. Looking south into Lorraine the hot May sun surrounded the curtains of pine trees with patches of light that joined in a great swath of colour at a forest ride.

The Cavalry troop were zig-zagging down this open space, set on a collision course with the line of panzers crawling along the paved road that followed the meanderings of the Semois River.

It seemed to Boden a breathtaking spectacle. There were at least thirty horsemen holding their carbines free of their holsters, the troopers' boots flashing below their baggy trousers and khaki greatcoats; each man's *burnous* tucked in at the neck below a blue and white striped *tcheka*. The brown leather of their shoulder straps and ammunition belts gleamed as brightly as the bandoliers below the white head ropes of the chargers, the flashing brass of the brow bands and curb bits and the crimson Moroccan saddles.

An NCO at the head of the column raised his carbine and a second later a shot rang out against the oily grey paintwork by the rear observation port, scratching the 14.5 mm armour to the left of Boden's elbow.

Over the intercom, Willy Wundshammer, the driver, gave a nervous laugh;

'That's the first time I've ever heard a shot in anger.'

As Willy spoke, Boden dropped to the level of the fighting compartment floor, his head and shoulders protected by the two vertical turret hatches.

'It won't be the last, either. Eyes front, and keep well away from that twenty metre drop on our right. If that's the worst the French can do, there won't be much to worry about.'

Wundshammer said;

'There must be something, road blocks, dragons' teeth, garlic mines. I think I see tree trunks every turn we come to.'

'Don't worry about it, there's only the Beau Geste cavalry.'

Seebohn, the Wireless Operator, who was crouched uncomfortably behind Boden in the tiny port compartment next to the engine radiator, said in the clipped, tense voice that got on both their nerves,

'What shall I do? Signal the Leutnant?'

Boden didn't bother to look at the nineteen year old who had announced to everyone in the troop that he intended to win an Iron Cross, after informing them that his uncle was a Gauleiter.

'No, Seebohn, our orders are to keep moving. And we won't stop to attack them either. You should know as well as I do that any crew switching off their engine will go on "Report".'

Seebohn didn't seem altogether satisfied with Boden's answer so he said, 'I think we should show a suitably aggressive spirit.'

'You can show what you like,' Boden replied. 'Flash them your Party card if you have to, but leave the command of the panzer to me.'

Boden forgot about Seebohn as the Mark 2 panzer ground up the increasing slope in second gear and the speed began to fall away from fifteen kmh The Unteroffizier looked up the forest ride to where the Spahis were plummeting down in irregular open order.

He guessed that the French patrol had spotted the long panzer column that wound back eighty kilometres to Germany, from the ridge above; but since his and the other panzers of 6 Platoon had been hidden by dead ground, they had been unobserved in the winding folds of the Semois Valley. Now that the French Commander had made his decision to gain the road, the impetus of the Cavalry Troop's descent made it impossible to adopt a more prudent course. And so it became inevitable that he would have to cross the lurching line of panzers and gain the doubtful protection of the slopes above the River Semois.

It was easy now to pick out the Commander wearing the ridged Adrian helmet of 1918, his scarlet and white cloak floating behind him as he waved his men forward with his sabre.

'I still can't believe it,' Boden said.

'That makes two of us,' Wundshammer said. 'I thought they only used horses to guard their President.'

'It's out of some old movie.'

'At least they've got guns. The panzers were charged by Polish Lancers at Wroclaw. Anyway I don't mind what they do so long as it isn't dangerous. I have a foreman machinist's job on the heavy lorries waiting for me in Neckar, once the war's over.'

Seebohn said intensely,

'It'll be all over by the Autumn, you'll see. The Führer has said so.'

Boden sighed. Seebohn always seemed to talk like an official bulletin. But the Wireless Operator hadn't finished.

'There'll still be enough time for us to give the Tommies a thrashing.'

Seebohn glanced round for approval, but Boden had hoisted himself back through the turret. The other two tanks of 6 Platoon were behind him, first Richter's and then Hagen's. It looked increasingly certain that Boden's panzer would become the object of the charge.

However, although all he had to do was duck down back into the fighting compartment, traverse the turret and operate the MG 34 to destroy them all, somehow it seemed vaguely unsporting.

By now there was little time left to make the kind of calculated decision he preferred, for the first wave of ragged cavalry had almost reached the road, striking sparks off the pave.

Instinctively he tugged his Walther .38 from the black leather holster on his left hip and, bracing his wrist against the shield in front of the turret hatch, took careful aim at the Officer, who was closely followed by a bugler carrying a blue and white pennant, and who repeatedly sounded the 'charge' against the grinding roar of the panzer's 140 hp Maybach engine.

Boden fired and the bullet grazed the Captain's calf, as he came on, slashing wildly at the Unteroffizier's head, before reining in at the impassable slope that led to the river.

However, the width of the portside hull made Boden an impossible target, so that the steel of the Frenchman's sabre only rang out against the deflection ridge below the turret. Boden fired a second shot at the French Officer who now galloped headlong down the verge against the flow of the panzer column towards the burning ruins of the Frontier post at Florenville.

Shots and ricochets spattered against the panzer's side armour as the Spahis hopelessly tried to bring the German column to a halt. For the time the French cavalry was unopposed, since the line of slow moving panzers masked each other. Although the onslaught of the Moroccan Spahis could only be described as suicidal, they had no choice, since a glance to the left was enough to tell the French Captain of the sheer drop to the Semois River and his decision to turn downhill into the advancing German column had decided the outcome some minutes before.

The Moroccan Spahis followed where he led, seething down the road in a confused and irrational body.

'Straight out of the history books,' Boden said as he watched the dustclouds raised by the cavalry on the verge; now that they were a hundred metres away down the road, he slipped his automatic back into its holster.

Seebohn turned and said critically,

'It was not necessary for you to allow that to happen; you could have gunned them down with the MG 34.'

'Why let it bother you, Seebohn? If they're intending to occupy the Third Reich, they've got to get past 28 odd Wehrmacht Divisions, before crossing the Rhine and planting their tricolour on the Brandenburg Gate.'

'We should have stopped them when they hit the road. It's an insult to let them come charging our line just as if the Emperor Napoleon was still running their show.'

Boden was silent for a moment, controlling his temper and reminding himself of Seebohn's obsession to avenge his father wounded on the Somme Battlefield in 1916 when the infantry were overrun by the primitive British tanks at Hamel. Then he said, 'If you don't mind, Seebohn, we'll leave the mopping up operation to the people behind. We've more important things to think about, such as getting into tank country.'

By now the momentum of the French Cavalry, disorderly as it was, had brought them to a hairpin where the road had been blasted out of the solid rock. As the panzer NCO watched them funnel into the narrow road cutting, he was reminded of brightly enamelled toy soldiers against the sober black uniforms and berets of the panzer crews and the dull grey paintwork of their tanks.

Then he picked out the sudden high pitched staccato of an MG 34, joined by a second and third in a sinister, deadly fugue, as on the far side of the bend, the following panzers, their field of fire now free, aimed their machine guns and interrupted the resonating bugle call.

At the same time the horsemen stopped abruptly, milling at the narrow opening as horses and riders wavered and crumpled under withering machine gun fire. Four Spahis dropped from their saddles, their impeccable uniforms torn to bloody tatters, and lay stretched out at incongruous angles while two of the chargers danced and whinnied uncertainly around them.

Other riderless horses began to canter back up the road as the French Captain vainly attempted to rally his troop and lead it anywhere away from the devastating machine gun fire.

However, at that moment, Captain Renouf of the fifth Moroccan Spahis received a burst of machine gun fire across his left thigh, as he tugged at his reins, breaking the femur and severing his left leg below the pelvis so that he began to slip off the right side of his horse. At that moment, however, his right foot became entangled with its stirrup, so that as he fell his charger, neighing in fear, dragged him along the road, his Adrian steel helmet scraping against the brown pave blocks. Captain Renouf still firmly grasped his sabre, while blood from his femoral artery jetted into the carnage of wounded and dying men and horses that surrounded him.

A second burst of machine gun fire stopped his charger, and, its dorsal cord severed, it collapsed with a broken back, as the great oblique externus muscle was slashed open and its intestines began to spill out.

The rest of the Spahis continued to mill round the bugler, uncertain as to what they were now expected to do. The bugler continued to sound the retreat as more men fell. The terrible screams of the wounded horses trampling their own viscera, and the desperate shouts of their unseated riders, added to the horrible inevitability of total annihilation as the approaching German panzers closed to point blank range at the hairpin bend.

Seebohn, suddenly sobered by this scene, exclaimed, 'The panzers aren't going to stop!'

Boden said, 'They have orders not to.'

Seebohn looked away. 'It would be better to have a bullet than to die like that.'

'Just be thankful you're not one of the ones that has to drive through that shambles.'

Wundshammer grimaced and said, 'I'm glad I've got my back to that grand guignol. When I was a boy I used to faint at the sight of blood. Anyway, Seebohn, if there's only cavalry between us and the sea you should thank the Führer for arranging things so well.'

'So long as we really teach the bastards a lesson this time.'

Wundshammer said, 'There'll be plenty of time to play heroes past the Maginot, at least we haven't been invited to make a frontal attack on that.'

As Boden climbed back through the turret hatch he strained his eyes ahead and pulled down his goggles because of the dust. Behind he heard the changing of gears as the panzers came to the hairpin. The sound was an undertone to the screams of the wounded and dying.

He said to Seebohn,

'That's war for you. You can tell me you won't take prisoners once we've made it to Calais. All I want is for this troop to get there first and win the race to the sea.'

2 Meuse Crossing

Outside Sedan on Route Nationale 64, Boden's panzer troop overtook two companies of infantry marching towards the invisible front line in the hot, late afternoon sunlight. With their pressed slate blue uniforms and gleaming black boots, they looked as though they were leaving the parade ground after Review except that they wore their gold eagle emblazoned steel helmets slung at their hips, their tunics were open necked and they were in battle order. As they marched, they sang:

'We'll soon be marching home
To our lovely Schwabia land,
We'll soon be marching home
And have finished the job in hand.'

Seebohn, who came from Wismar in Mecklenburg on the Baltic, commented sourly, 'Those southerners are as bad as the Italians; all they can do is sing and look pretty.'

Wundshammer said, 'Soon we'll be listening to a different tune.'

As the Mark 2 panzer approached Sedan, Boden caught sight of the brooding, rectangular fort that guarded the river, high above the Meuse. Below it hung a pall of smoke that rumbled and flashed red. Boden had not noticed the whine of the Stukas because of the constant roar of the engine.

Boden said, 'There go the Bertas.'

High above in the cloudless sky hung a circle of Stukas. One by one, in turn, they screamed down, their sirens wailing, to release their 250 kilogramme bombs into the tormented smoke cloud.

Wundshammer asked, 'Are we detailed for target practice?'

Boden replied, 'We've got the flag out at the back. Anyway, it looks as though they're leaving.'

As the latest Junkers 87 rejoined the circus, the leader shook his angled wings and made off eastwards.

'Going back to refuel and rearm and find another target.'

Wundshammer said, 'You've almost convinced me.'

'France'll collapse like a pack of cards under that kind of treatment,' Seebohn added.

Wundshammer laughed, 'There speaks the optimist.'

Now that the dive bombers had left, they could hear the distant crash of shells within the perimeter of the burning town, together with intermittent bursts of machine gun fire.

Wundshammer said; 'At least there's a diversion away from that inferno.'

A blue and white sign marked ST QUENTIN had been attached to the latticework of a leaning French Power pylon. Underneath somebody had scrawled: TO THE CHANNEL – CALAIS NEXT STOP.

Boden said, 'Those Stukas were probably plastering the far side of the river.'

As they passed Direction Control the Feldgendarmerie Sergeant with his silver gorget shouted up to Boden,

'Keep your head down, soldier. There are snipers, and there's no time to bury you.'

Boden gave him a party salute.

Five minutes later Wundshammer turned into the Rue Rovigo which ran parallel to the Meuse, crushing a tram wire pole and churning over a heap of masonry from a collapsed house front. The upper bedroom had survived intact and through the smoke it was possible to make out a brass bedstead with a pink counterpane. Behind, Boden heard the roar of two BMW motorbikes.

Seebohn said, 'Here's the riot squad to flush out the snipers.'

The road looked empty ahead as the Mark 2 panzer's tracks crunched over the broken glass that carpeted the pave. Besides the leather coated driver, each bike carried two machine gunners, both armed with an MG 34 on the combination. As the two motorbikes entered the street in parallel, the number one gunner on each combination blasted the ground floor windows of the houses, while his number two, holding his machine gun at an angle of forty-five degrees, methodically hosed the upper windows. As they disappeared into the distance, Seebohn said, 'That's the way to clean shit from the street.'

A third of the way down the Rue Rovigo, Boden noticed a sudden, jerky movement above a baker's shop, where the stream of machine gun fire had shattered the plate glass window and sent the long French loaves spinning across the marble topped counter. A moment later a rifle rattled down onto the criss-cross pavement below. As the panzer passed by, Boden could see the body of a French infantryman drooping out of the window above, his horizon blue uniform soaked with blood below his tilted Adrian helmet. Blood from the hole in his chest ran across the faded shop board obliterating the owner's name after BOULANGERIE.

Further on they came to the bodies of two Senegalese Colonial troops still grasping their 1895 rifles. One of them, who was headless in dark blue overalls and puttees, had been attempting to slide on his bayonet at the moment of death.

Seebohn pulled a face. 'You can rely on the French to use primitives.'

Boden ignored the remark.

The buildings lining the Avenue General Margueritte were on fire as they entered the Northern suburb of the town, but since there was little wind the flames tended to travel vertically, dispersing the smoke, although they were fierce enough to set the rows of plane trees lining the Avenue ablaze.

They passed a horse butcher's, its gold painted horse head as yet untouched by the flames. Boden caught the sooty stench of roasting carcasses and felt sick, his stomach tightening. It reminded him of a smell he knew from Poland: that from a burning tank with a trapped crew.

Seebohn said, 'Almost time for lunch.'

'There's no time for anything until we get across the river.'

Boden tried to forget the stories he had heard about the

French tanks with their heavy guns and armour. The Renault Char B mounted a 75 mm gun that could slice through the light 30 mm glacis armour of the Mark 2 panzers like a knife through butter.

He recalled that at the final briefing Leutnant Von Dressen had given the vaguest and yet somehow the most alarming of orders.

'We are advancing west. On no account are you to stop.'

'West's a big objective, Herr Leutnant. We could end up in England now that we've been fixed up with water wings to swim the Channel.'

Boden had seen the steel flotation barges that fitted round the panzer hulls at an ordnance railhead near Trier.

'Don't get too excited; our first task is to get across the Meuse if that's any kind of consolation.'

'Everyone knows that valley's almost impregnable. Look at the forts at Eben Emael.'

'Yes, Boden and the Fallschirmjagern took them in an afternoon.'

'However, after that the French will be waiting for us.'

'As usual the French will be in chaos; it's the way they like to do things. At that point their front consists of two of the lousiest Reservist Divisions they could manage to scrape together. They've very little in the way of support weapons either. Fortress troops. Forty five year olds who can't run a hundred metres without risking a coronary.'

'I still think it's a tough nut to crack – tougher than Poland.'

'That wouldn't be difficult. Anyway, the French always tell everybody what they want them to believe about their impregnable Maginot Line. This time they've hypnotised themselves with their own propaganda.'

'Well I certainly believe in their heavy artillery, and their panzers aren't half bad either.'

Von Dressen smiled his superior Officer's smile that he kept in reserve against abysmal ignorance.

'Quite right, except that they tuck their guns away under twenty feet of concrete and spread their tanks along their entire front to support their infantry. None of their General

Staff seem to think the reserve Divisions ahead of us even qualify for that luxury.'

Boden clenched his hands behind his back until the knuckles were white, as he always did in moments of uncertainty.

'It sounds much too simple to me; all this pressing on into the unknown.'

'The Channel's the obvious objective. Rommel has been sending down directives for days emphasising that we've got to keep on the move. There may be one or two setbacks, but I want everybody in the Platoon to co-operate. However, you can tell the panzer boys that the first tank from our Platoon that reaches the white cliffs of Calais will qualify for a week's leave in Paris, all expenses paid. Tabarin, Moulin Rouge, Ladies; the full works. What do you think about that?'

'Provided we all make it, that sounds a good idea to me. They'll all be glad to hear they may win a bonus.'

'God, Boden, why are you always so bloody cautious?'

'It's the result of being born in the heart of the country, Herr Leutnant. One's never quite sure which way things are going to go.'

* * *

By now, Boden's panzer had come to an area of burning storage depots by the Cloth Mills along the Meuse. The Feldgendarmerie arrows still pointed persistently North to what must be the bridgehead but all they could see was an approaching bottleneck packed with Ten Division's motor transport passing Sedan along Route Nationale 77 from the North. There were more indications of battle now that the road ran along the riverside; the bodies of five camouflage smocked assault troops lay floating face downwards in a bed of smouldering reeds, beside a punctured and shrivelled black assault dinghy. Boden noted that their heads were tilted under water with the weight of their steel helmets.

On the bank above stood a burned out French ambulance resting on its axles, its silver bell still hanging from the steel struts lining the cab roof. From time to time it rang from the shockwave of a not-so-distant shell burst.

Wundshammer changed down as he came to the traffic jam, and Boden said, 'Who told you to do that? Keep moving.'

'It's getting pretty crowded.'

'So'll hell be on judgement day. We've been told to keep going, remember? If those other buggers don't clear out of the way in time, that's their bad luck.'

Wundshammer revved the Maybach and changed up reluctantly.

The panzer lurched forward to the left of a stationary half-track blocking the road as it swerved to avoid a French Citroen with a shattered windscreen and a line of machine gun holes across the bonnet.

As the Rhinelander changed direction, the panzer crashed against the side of an Sfz 231 armoured car carrying the double white cross markings of Sixth Panzer, below the black, white and red swastika command flag of the General Staff.

Boden saw that it was a Staff Signals vehicle, the aerial running back over the sloping hull like permanent hand-rails. The driver of the armoured car braked and swore at them above the roar of his Bussing engine as he was forced to let them through. Inside Boden momentarily glimpsed the flat, olive green caps of Staff Officers.

'Move it, before they tell us to stop!' he shouted to Wundshammer.

'Don't blame me, it's not my fault we're in this foul-up.'

'I didn't say it was.'

As Wundshammer eased back the right hand steering lever, the Mark 2 panzer rocked against the double mud-guards and carved a long sliver of steel out of the side of the armoured car.

Seebohn said;

'And we handle those Colonial Cavalry with kid gloves.'

Boden said impatiently;

'Same thing, different problem, we've got to keep moving.'

Two minutes later they were were waved impatiently on and into the middle of the road by two feldgendarmes on motorbikes, past the burned out shell of a house, its windowless outer wall painted with a huge advertisement for RIPOLIN in royal blue, pink and black. The faded paint had bubbled and peeled from the heat of the fire within.

The receiver crackled and Seebohn turned and said, 'Von Dressen's getting an earful from some Army General for that bit of reckless driving, and he doesn't sound too happy about it.'

Boden said,

'That's his bad luck.'

'So long as it isn't ours. Now they're threatening to pack Wundshammer back to Driving School.'

'There's nothing I'd enjoy more, except the food isn't very good. I am looking forward to French cuisine.'

'If you get any fatter you won't be able to make it through the hatch.'

'Anyway,' said Boden, 'I'd miss his corny Rhineland sense of humour.'

Wundshammer laughed.

'I can see my jokes will be the death of me. Where's my pay book, I'll leave my bread bag to you in my will for that.'

Boden said,

'In any case all that General's doing is pulling rank. Fighting Units have priority even over the Staff. He wasn't controlling a battle or doing anything of interest to us from what I could see.'

By this time they were bumping through the countryside over a shell-torn, uneven road beside banks of heavy, lush summer vegetation. To the left Boden could now make out the Meccano-like structure of the CM bridge that the pioneers had only just finished, floating on pontoons across the Meuse.

Two pontoon trailers had been left beside the bank, its red earth torn by shell holes, in front of the line of elms that cut across the earth track to the bridgehead. A Renault light tractor had overturned its chenillette ammunition trailer, and a heap of brass cased 7.5 rounds was scattered among the mole hills. The red, white and blue French identification target gleamed on the right hand dome of the hull, surrounded by the swollen carcases of dead cows.

'Someone's scored a bull's eye,' Wundshammer said, but nobody laughed. A cloud of flies buzzed noisily above the hive-like visors of the twin domes, and Boden was relieved that they did not have to see what had happened to the crew. Wundshammer lost his smile as he caught the stench of the decaying cows and felt the tension rising at what might be in store for them on the other side of the river.

The heights beyond the Meuse reared up ahead of them, dominating the river from a distance of a mile. It seemed to Boden an ideal position for heavy artillery.

The pontoons bucked under the ten ton weight of the Mark 2 panzer as Wundshammer slowly edged across the swaying bridge. Another Feldgendarme waved them impatiently on beside the wooden signboard he obviously took with him everywhere which read THE ENEMY IS AHEAD.

Then they crossed the meadow beyond the river, their tracks creasing the thick lush grass.

Seebohn, riding on the back of the panzer, pointed into the clear blue sky beyond the trees and shouted,

'It looks like our boys are getting ready to give them another pasting.'

Wundshammer squinted up through the driver's port.

'They could be 110s or even Italian; maybe the Duce's made up his mind at last.'

High above them at ten thousand feet, the little black silhouette crosses suddenly sparkled as the sunlight caught their long narrow canopies.

Boden was puzzled.

'I don't recognise them; they can't be ours.'

'Who else is there?' Wundshammer said. 'We've never set eyes on the Frog Air Force, only Stukas.'

'Just keep going,' Boden said between his teeth.

One by one the twenty flashing silhouettes fell away from the sun, plunging down in a long, noiseless dive which would bring them upstream of the pontoon Boden's panzer had just crossed. As they approached at four hundred kilometres an hour, Boden could see from the deep brown and green camouflage and their yellow-ringed red, white and blue roundels that they were British medium bombers.

'What the hell are they?'

Boden shrugged, struggling to recall the appropriate recognition silhouette.

Seebohn said,

'They must be Fairey Battles. I've seen them on patrol this side of the Siegfried Line.'

'A long way from Piccadilly.'

'Their base was at Reims, that's close enough for us.'

Through the trees on the other side of the river, Boden began to hear the mechanical clatter of the 20 cm Quad Flak guns opening up from their self-propelled 'Furniture Vans', their turret armour square and unwieldy, as the Panzer Division's Flak guns put up a belated defence that sent flak bursts crowding up into the clear blue sky at the rate of four a second.

However, this did nothing to discourage the Battles from trying to reach the Meuse Bridges that were their target, including the pontoon that Boden's panzer had just crossed. A five hundred pound bomb exploded in the river, casting up a gout of frothing water, to be followed by a second and a third. Boden's eardrums crackled at the shock waves.

The leading Battle suddenly banked away from the flak and began to follow the unmade road they had just taken from the edge of the Meuse.

The next five hundred pound bomb landed to the left and behind them, throwing up a jet of smoking red earth and cordite which sent stones and debris rattling against the side armour of the Mark 2 panzer.

Richter's panzer, which immediately followed them, rocked on its suspension as the rear gunner of the first Fairey Battle began to fire round after round of .303 from his twin Vickers at the back of the canopy. As the plane stormed over their heads at fifty feet, Boden quite clearly made out the bomber's crew, leather helmeted and overalled in the broad, white webbing of their parachute harness.

The second wing of Battles followed the first, ploughing up the field with machine gun fire, but not doing any more effective damage.

Seebohn said,

'The Air Staff aren't half getting excited with the Luftwaffe and quite right too. It's not at all efficiently arranged. They want to know what the hell's going on. The excuse is that the MEs are engaging Spitfires over Holland and the rest of the winged wonders are busy protecting our Heinkels on targets behind the line.'

'That makes me feel really good,' Boden said. 'Hullo, here we go again.'

Having gained height, the Battles swept round in a southerly arc, sending bursts of tracer into the lines of Wehrmacht transport crowding the road along the Eastern bank of the Meuse. Suddenly a heavy servicing truck carrying two thousand litres of fuel exploded with a roar, throwing out gouts of flaming petrol to the middle of the river.

By now the Mark 2 panzer had almost arrived at the far end of the meadow, but there was no cover, and in their exposed position there was no alternative but to thrust through the hedge and follow the rough track that the panzers ahead had ploughed through the green summer corn.

Seebohn was clearly not enjoying this first battle experience, although he put a bold enough face upon it.

'Why don't we make for cover?'

'What cover?'

There was a line of elm trees in the field beyond at the next ridge, but other than that only the poplar trees beside the river.

'Any cover, for God's sake, under the panzer even.'

'You'll just have to sweat it out, Seebohn. Jump out and run, if you think it'll do you any good, I'm not stopping you. Maybe they'll put you in for an Iron Cross.'

Seebohn, clearly stung by the remark, decided to make no move.

Even as Boden finished speaking, a stream of fire from one of the attacking Battles smacked against their rear armour whining this way and that in a crescendo of ricochets. Although they could not penetrate the 30 mm slanted steel Boden felt impotent and naked at being unable to return their fire.

The panzer behind vanished momentarily under a shower of exploding earth as another bomber released its load.

Wundshammer said,

'That's Richter behind, poor sod.'

The panzer lurched towards the trees with damage to the track beside the port idler wheel. When Richter reached cover the engine stopped and he jumped out with the rest of the crew to inspect the damage.

The Observer in the Battle obviously sensed a possible victory, for the bomber turned sharply to bear down on the stationary target.

'Bloody idiot,' said Boden. 'He should have kept going. Give him a shout on the platoon net.'

But as he spoke a *Kette* of black winged ME 109s skimmed over the trees, dropping almost to ground level.

The Battle's pilot realised his mistake fifteen seconds too late as he tried to gain height and change track by returning to the Meuse. As he began to climb clumsily towards the pontoon bridge the left hand ME 109 made a pass and overtook him, the explosive shells of his 20 mm cannon ripping along the narrow fuselage of the Battle so that its single Merlin engine began to stutter and cough, and, after flying unsteadily for a hundred metres, it fell slowly away towards the ground, a long smoke trail streaming from the starboard exhaust.

The remaining nineteen Fairey Battles immediately climbed away, now only too fully aware that they could not compete with the marauding trio of fighters that could jink across the sky at half their speed again. As the Battles slowly gained altitude, the fighter flight returned again and again to the attack. Soon there were a further six black smoke trails criss-crossing the sky.

Another Battle, caught with its bombload, exploded in mid air, leaving vanishing wisps that spiralled out from the falling debris. Then the shattered squadron of Medium

Bombers reeled away, soon lost in the peaceful May landscape of the Meuse, with its lush green fields and poplars, disappearing west into a cloudless blue sky.

Wundshammer said,

'So much for the R.A.F. They fight with obsolete aircraft. Very brave.'

The black winged ME 109BF flipped into a Victory Roll before heading back over the Ardennes for Trier as Seebohn said,

'The Herr Leutnant wants you.' He said it in such a way so that it was insolent to both Boden and Von Dressen.

Boden climbed into the cramped space of the fighting compartment since it could mean that there was a target ahead.

'Right, Seebohn, put him on.'

His headphones crackled as Seebohn switched from the intercom.

'Yes Herr Leutnant? Boden here.'

'You'll have to have a word with that well-built driver of yours. The Herr General didn't appreciate having his paintwork scratched.' Von Dressen's voice came over the set as a lazy drawl as though they were out on manoeuvres at Nuremburg Tank School.

'You gave us our orders, that armoured car was in the way.'

'That's not how I heard it. However the General respects your keenness and devotion to duty even though on this occasion it appears to have been misplaced. He's asked me personally to assign you and your crew to a special task.'

Boden's heart sank; that could only mean they were about to be involved in something that was messy, unpleasant and dangerous. In any event they could now wave goodbye to a week in Paris. Before he spoke he realised that some busybody Staff Officer could be listening in to see how he was going to take it.

'It's an honour to have been selected.'

'I'm glad you're taking it like that Boden, but it'll hold you up, I'm afraid.'

'Well, Herr Leutnant, we're not the only ones.'

Von Dressen pulled in his breath.

'Has something happened I don't know about? Has anybody been hit?'

'Nothing really serious, Herr Leutnant. Richter's panzer has had its bolts loosened thanks to a Tommy bomb, but it's nothing serious. They're out behind in the spring corn replacing the track plates and putting in a new link.'

'Well, the whole platoon's under a handicap in that case. Anyway, you're ordered to support an Assault Company that's been detailed to neutralise a fort five kilometres to the south.'

'I thought we'd got through the Maginot once we had passed Sedan.'

'We have and we haven't. The French have constructed strongpoints west from Montmédy. Generally the order is to drive round, but this time you've been specially detailed to join the Fire Brigade.'

'That'll really be the end of the sitzkrieg for us then?'

'The General admires Wundshammer's road manners so much you've to join the Hessen boys at Flize; that's the next village. Cheer up, it may not take all that long. The fort's just over the hill from there, but you'll have to wait, it's scheduled to be a night attack.'

'Anything you say, Herr Leutnant.'

'Anything the Herr General says, Boden. He sends his best wishes and hopes there won't be any unseen French 75s lurking about to crease your mudguards.'

* * *

Wundshammer had heard this conversation and was upset by the sudden turn of events, feeling in some way to blame. He was also sensitive to the Leutnant's snide remark about his figure.

'Another millimetre to the left and I'd have been all right.'

Seebohn said sourly,

'You should fine tune your steering, Wundshammer. I like to be on the winning team. Bang goes a week on the loose in Paris.'

Wundshammer shouted,

'What do you know about it? Why don't you go hiking with the Hitler Youth, that's much more your line. What right have you got to criticise my driving? I was only doing what I was told!'

Boden said,

'I'm afraid that kind of argument never impresses Officers.'

Seebohn said sourly,

'It's just typical of you, Wundshammer, to be worrying about laying the Parisian poules. Still, it's not to be wondered at – you Rhinelanders are really half French anyway, not German at all when one comes to think about it.'

Wundshammer became even more incensed at what he considered to be Seebohn's unjustified attack.

'Cut it out Seebohn, you should have stayed in Mecklenburg, gutting herrings, then after a bit they'd have presented you with a toy U-Boat to play with in your bath.'

Seebohn got mad at this.

'You know damn well we're an army family, not only that my uncle was on the Blood March.'

'Cut it out, Seebohn, we've all heard that record often enough.'

'Why can't you ever stop joking, you fat slob. All you ever do is prance about like some Koblenz Carnival clown who's pretending to get the grapes in. With you at the wheel it's more than likely we'll drop into the first tank trap we come to.'

Boden began to wonder whether Seebohn's outburst was sparked off by the prospect of approaching action, so he said,

'We can worry about that when we hit the Maginot.'

At the end of the next field they caught up with the forward company of an Infantry Regiment in half-track armoured carriers, just as they were turning south onto a secondary road. The yellow and blue road sign established that they were only a kilometre and a half away from Flize. Wundshammer said,

'There was no need to have brought a map. They've even signposted it for us.'

Boden gazed ahead.

'That looks like our Infantry outfit.'

The Assault troops wore steel helmets and battle order. The pioneers carried flame thrower packs on their knees, and poles for concentric charges stuck out over the back of the armour. One by one, as the troop carriers came down the hill and entered the village, they came to a halt in the Square and switched off their engines. Two sections immediately formed up before racing to take posts at the street corners, while the howitzer section brought forward their 37 mm anti-tank gun and wheeled it into position to cover the main road south.

Boden was impressed by the speed with which this was all done.

'Switch off the bloody engine, Wundshammer, so I can hear myself think.'

When the thudding of the transmission slowly melted away and he heard the faint noise of the wood pigeons in the belfry of the village church, Boden felt the novelty of silence drifting over him. It was only then that he realised they had been on the move for sixteen hours, re-fuelling on the move from the stock of jerricans they carried.

Looking around him, he could see that the village of Flize chiefly consisted of the buildings built round the Square in which they were now standing. The Square was narrow and oblong, flanked on each side by pink, lime washed houses.

However, although the shop windows were shuttered and barred, it seemed evident that there had already been some looting. Two shop fronts had been blown out with grenades, for the shutters hung on their hinges before the shattered plate glass. There seemed to be no logic in why they had been particularly chosen. One was a milliner's where lengths of cloth had been discarded in the street; the second was a general goods store behind a cast iron pissoir, where fishing rods, a tennis racket and dozens of cans of pâté were now sprinkled across the outside pavement. Next to the church, further down the square, the doors of the Estaminet had been forced open and forty litre demi-johns of wine in wicker covered stone bottles had been lined up like ninepins at the edge of the gutter and used for target practice so that wine was still dribbling down onto the pave.

But there was no sign of life in the village and Boden could see no people. No one, that is, except for a feldgendarme on a motorbike who had been waiting for their arrival. Then the Unteroffizier saw the Leutnant commanding the Infantry Company climb down the angled side of the troop carrier and walk over to the feldgendarme who was holding a copy of the Michelin Guide. The officer waved to Boden to come over.

'Yes Herr Leutnant?'

The Leutnant was slightly older than Boden, perhaps twenty two, and wore steel rimmed glasses.

There was something deceptively academic about him, although he wore the ribbon of the War Merit Cross tucked discreetly round the top button of his tunic.

'My name is Ebbing. I'm in command of the assault team. What is your name?'

'Boden, Unteroffizier Boden.'

Ebbing stared at him as though trying to gauge his character with insufficient time. Then he smiled.

'Have an Eckstein, Unteroffizier Boden.'

Boden was grateful for a cigarette after the confinement in the tank.

'You're the crew that bumped into the General after lunch?'

'Yes, that's why we've been assigned to special duty with you.'

Ebbing smiled.

'It could happen to anyone where there's no traffic control; it's just your bad luck you tangled with a General.'

Boden had reached the conclusion that Ebbing did not seem too bad for a young officer, even though he spoke with a nasal Potsdamer accent that Boden couldn't be sure wasn't assumed.

'So, we are your specialists.'

'I rather thought that, Herr Leutnant.'

'Not quite the way you're thinking, we've all of us been in action before.'

'I was in Poland for a few weeks.'

'Good, so you'll know what it can be like. My company was Condor Legion in Spain, propping up the Black Flames and the rest of the Duce's men in Valencia. Blowing up the bridges when the Republicans started treading on their heels. We got back last June. You must have read about it.'

'There isn't much time to read the papers when you're constantly training.'

'Well this time we don't have any gallant allies to bail out, so we can tread on the heels of the French instead.'

'We seem to be doing that all right.'

'Yes, but tonight, Herr Unteroffizier, we're going to kick in the back door of that fort; see the hill over there to the south behind the church? There, to the left?'

'Yes, Herr Leutnant.'

'That's the fort, where the garrison are playing cards several metres below ground. They haven't fired on us, either because they don't know we're here, which is more than likely, or because their 75s are designed to traverse, or because they're waiting for orders. From what I've seen I should say the last was the most likely explanation, in which case time is on our side.'

'Yes, Herr Leutnant.'

'Your job will be to get round the other side of the hill to the West.'

'What do we have to do then?'

'We'll kick the doors down. Forts like that usually have steel laminated plate doors up to 100 mm to let them out on leave with a little light railway.'

'That's quite a thickness, I doubt whether I'd be able to achieve any noticeable damage with my 2 cm.'

'Don't worry about it. We're all here to help each other. In case, for example, the garrison wakes up and starts shooting off machine guns at my boys. Once you see my white success rocket, you're free to be on your way; free to go paddling or making sandcastles or whatever else you want to do when you get to the seaside. There won't be any fun like that in store for us, we'll be stuck around here de-lousing the Maginot.'

The Leutnant extracted two waxy pink bricks from the private's breadbag he was carrying.

'Here, Unteroffizier, catch.'

'What are they?'

'Don't worry, the primers come separately.'

Boden eyed the blocks of Hexogen explosive he was now holding without any great enthusiasm.

'Now run along and relax for a bit. We won't start moving across open ground until dusk. I'll send a patrol forward to see there isn't anything nasty or unexpected.'

'That's very kind of you, Herr Leutnant. Can we expect the Goulash Canon before we make the assault? I'd like to think we're on your ration strength.'

'I daresay it could be arranged. Have a word with my Sergeant.'

'It's not for me particularly, it's for the driver who did the damage. It'll make him feel better, especially if he's going to have to career cross country on his headlights.'

'That's right, Boden, always put your men first, it's usually a good investment.'

Ebbing turned away and began to walk towards the church tower to inspect the night's objective while Boden returned to the Mark 2 panzer.

Seebohn was sprawled beside the turret, fiddling with the rod aerial. Wundshammer seemed to be asleep.

'What's all that about?' Seebohn asked.

'Briefing for tonight's attack.'

'If it's all the same to you, I think I'll do some window shopping, and I won't need my wallet.' He patted his hip pocket that everyone knew was thick with big denomination Reichmark notes. None of them could understand why he had to carry so much money except to show off.

'While I'm about it, I'll supplement our iron rations. After our Home Front Austerity programme I've almost forgotten what a bar of chocolate looks like.'

3 Maginot

When it got too dark for Wundshammer to continue maintenance effectively, Boden came back to the panzer.

He had examined the ground that led to the back of the fort after listening to the report made by Ebbing's patrol. So far as they were able to see, there were no mines or tank obstacles, although it had been impossible to reconnoitre the entrance which they were planning to attack.

Ebbing joined Boden as Wundshammer put away his tool box and inspection lamp. Wundshammer was sweating, as he usually did after the least kind of exertion.

'You've mapped out your route, then?' Ebbing enquired.

'Up the road to the farm that's marked "Les Cheniers" on the map and then a trip across country by the direct route. I should get there in about fifteen minutes, barring accidents.'

'You said yourself you've checked out all the obstacles and you were satisfied.'

'Only personally as far as the farm, since I didn't want to risk advertising our arrival in advance. However, having fought through the Polish Campaign I doubt whether everything will go quite as smoothly as if we were out on manoeuvres.'

Ebbing stared at him thoughtfully.

'It'd better.'

'Oh it will Herr Leutnant. Don't worry about that.'

'I've been busy as well. I've laid on a surprise fire shoot with the 150 mm howitzers at Division. So we must be in position at 21.15 hrs. That should keep their eyes front. There'll also be other surprises, harassing fire from a battery of 105 mm up to that time, and I've managed to get the co-operation of the Luftwaffe.'

'Sounds as though we've had our work cut out.'

'I believe in being thorough.'

'Won't the French put out patrols?'

'It's not likely if you ask me, but if they want to there's nothing my men enjoy more than a game of hide and seek in the dark.'

Boden glanced over to where Ebbing's men were checking their hand grenades and explosives, tossing the primed explosives one to another like tennis balls.

'They look tough enough.'

'They are, I can assure you of that.'

As the Leutnant finished speaking a shell roaring like a distant express tore through the dusk and exploded on the forward hill slope of the fort.

'There goes the first round,' Ebbing remarked, and smiled.

'I'll start moving up, Herr Leutnant,' Boden said.

Wundshammer switched on the engine as Boden climbed in, and the Unteroffizier immediately noticed the hot, sweet smell of engine oil emanating from the engine housing to his right. As the panzer began to move, Boden thought he could hear the slap of petrol against the side of the starboard tank.

'How are we off for fuel?'

Wundshammer looked serious for a moment and turned his head, creasing the rolls of flesh at the back of his neck.

'All the reserve cans are exhausted. There's a hundred and forty seven litres in the tank. That should see us through a hundred kilometres.'

Boden slipped back into the fighting compartment, ducking to avoid the breach support of the 2 cm Kwk 30 for a moment wondering how it was possible for Wundshammer to squeeze through the driver's hatch and down into the narrow seat. He decided that it was not altogether important, although Wundshammer inevitably drew adverse comment on parade from Von Dressen who was constantly sending him off round the grenadier training course wearing full battle order. It was not done maliciously.

'Look here, Wundshammer, it's for your own good. You're a trained soldier now. I'm surprised they were able to fix you up with a uniform.'

'Begging to report, Herr Leutnant, it was specially tailored.'

Von Dressen adjusted Wundshammer's Field Cap so that the silver embroidered badge was centred on his forehead.

'Well, you look like a tank man. I can't complain about your turnout. I'm just worried about your health.'

'Begging to report, Herr Leutnant, the M.O. has given me a clean bill of health. Tells me I'll probably live to be a hundred.'

'I doubt that very much, if you have to make a rapid exit from a burning panzer. Or maybe you'd like to be fried alive?'

'Begging to report, Herr Leutnant, I'm never checked when we practise abandon.'

This was perfectly true. It was one of the miracles of nature that in a matter of seconds Wundshammer could pour his enormous bulk out of the hatch above his head as effortlessly as a cork leaving a champagne bottle.

'Well, Wundshammer, I'm not satisfied. If you're so fit, it won't do you any harm to lose a few kilos round the battle course.'

'Ja-wohl, Herr Leutnant,' Wundshammer used to shout, and double back to the barracks to put on his spotlessly kept boots, pouches, belt, leather braces, gas mask, entrenching tool, bayonet, bread bag, canteen, cape and mess cans. All of which would require two hours' attention that evening.

It made no difference however. When Wundshammer had returned, pink cheeked and muddy, he immediately cleaned all of his equipment and then made off to the Canteen to down a string of Lowenbrau Steins which more than replaced what the imposed athletics had removed.

In spite of this blemish on his military character, Wundshammer was still the best mechanic in the Regiment which was why Boden was so fond of him.

Wundshammer tapped the petrol gauge and said,

'We shouldn't need any more tonight.'

Boden said,

'Don't use up any more than you have to; once we're dismissed here I'm planning on taking the nearest road west.'

Wundshammer's frame shook as he laughed.

'Once we've redeemed ourselves in the eyes of the Herr General.'

'I don't mind taking orders from Von Dressen, but on the whole I want to avoid private wars and unknown details.'

'I'm with you there entirely.'

As the tracks clattered over the pave blocks, the Maybach whining in low gear, Boden became aware that Seebohn was, for once, unusually silent, and he kept fiddling with the FU 6 Frequency dial as though he was afraid that he might lose the link with Ebbing.

'Something gone wrong?' Boden asked him.

In the dim light inside the Fighting Compartment Boden now saw that Seebohn's face was white and his hands trembled as he crouched over the receiver.

'It's just that never having been in action before, I'm not sure how I'm going to react.'

'It'll all be over before you know it, believe me.'

Seebohn's attempted smile changed to a grimace.

'The trouble is I've an Iron Cross First Class to live up to. It was awarded to my father at Hamel.'

'So you told me, but I shouldn't worry too much about that. Nobody else here's interested in glory, so you'll only be competing against yourself.'

Seebohn's expression froze to wooden disbelief.

'But you should be! German honour demands it. That's not an attitude I'm used to.'

Wundshammer, who had heard this discussion over the intercom, interrupted to say,

'Just be your natural, smiling self, Seebohn, the one we all know and love so much. Sit back and enjoy the sound of the passing shells; it'll be your biggest thrill since you watched the herring boats sail in.'

Seebohn appealed to Boden.

'See what I mean, Unteroffizier? Always making jokes. It's enough to put anyone off. War's no laughing matter.'

Wundshammer said,

'Just stuff one of your chocolate bars in your mouth before my engine melts it.'

The results of Seebohn's foraging were stacked by the fan, next to the cold air intake.

'I think I will.'

'Good, there's nothing better for calming the nerves.'

Boden noticed that the nearer they came to the firing line the more relaxed Wundshammer became but the more tension Seebohn generated.

'I think it must be the dark,' Seebohn said after he had eaten two chocolate bars. 'That's what puts me off.'

'Well, at least they can't see us.'

'No, but surely they can hear us; with that fat swine Wundshammer taking us to nowhere, Christ knows where we'll end up.'

The intervals between the exploding rounds of harassing fire suddenly grew less as Boden heard the distant hum of bombers.

'What the hell's that?' Seebohn asked edgily.

'Heinkels, by the sound of it.'

'Christ, we've been bombed once today already.'

'Then you'll have some idea of what it's like, won't you?'

Boden was starting to get irritated by Seebohn's constant nervous comments as he stood in the turret trying to make out exactly where they were going. All he could see as they advanced down the farm lane to Les Cheniers were the silhouettes of isolated poplars, lit up momentarily by the flicker of explosions.

'We better start crossing the fields,' he said to Wundshammer.

The tank slewed left as Wundshammer quickly changed down and pulled at the left hand steering lever. The nose of the Mark 2 panzer dipped down suddenly, throwing Boden against the turret hatch padding. Glancing back, Boden thought he could see the shadowy figures of the following infantry. The night air was cold against his face.

As they moved through the standing crops that filled the field, the light of exploding bombs lit the hill fort and the landscape to the south. Once Boden caught sight of the steel hemisphere of a fortress turret and was puzzled why there seemed to be no active flak defences.

Boden checked the compass bearing once more as they began to climb a gradual slope.

'O.K., Wundshammer, you can keep on the present course.'

Then they crossed a ditch and began to run across what seemed levelled ground. The panzer rocked as Boden felt the double bump of the light railway tracks.

Seebohn looked round anxiously and announced,

'We're running into a tank trap.'

The panzer moved on.

'No, Seebohn,' Boden said patiently, 'that was only the light railway. Turn left and follow it up the slope, Wundshammer.'

This would bring them up to the heavy gates at the back of the Fort. The Rhinelander changed down and followed the dimly shining tracks up the hillside. Looking into the darkness ahead, Boden was aware of the dark horizontal wall of the fort.

'Put on the headlights.'

'Is that wise?' Seebohn asked.

'There's no point in scratching the paintwork, is there?' He glanced at his watch. The time was 21.12.

The panzer juddered as it crossed a junction in the light railway line and Wundshammer switched on the headlights to reveal a twenty metre blank stone wall embedded in the hillside, with an arch dead ahead which led through a tunnel to the principal works beyond. Wundshammer was so occupied with what lay in front that he did not see the cement mixer on their right as the starboard trackguard crunched into it and tilted it over.

Wundshammer said,

'Ebbing was wrong, there's no need to kick in this particular door, it's already open. They're still in the course of construction.'

Boden whistled.

'There's not even a guard post.'

Now, the headlights picked out a wooden signboard that read: CHANTIERS DE L'EST. ENTREPRISES M. FERNAY ET FILS.

Boden saw Ebbing dart across the shadows.

'Put out that light.'

At the sound of his voice a machine gun began to fire from the casemate on the right.

Seebohn said,

'They've spotted us now. That was aimed at us.'

'So what?' Boden said between his teeth. 'Did you think they'd toss us a bunch of flowers or something?'

Boden depressed the traverse lever and swung the turret to starboard as Wundshammer dimmed the headlights and edged the panzer back into the shadow of the wall that ran at right angles from the archway ahead. At the same time he was aware of the crash of artillery beyond the hill and to the east.

To the right of the entrance to the casemate he could dimly make out the flashes of the Chatellrault machine gun as it raked the open ground in front of the panzer. Boden looked carefully through the sight once more, marking the tracer flash, then he stretched out his hand out for the 2 cm magazine that clipped on to the left of the breech to see that it was secure.

Seebohn said,

'We won't get very far with armour piercing.'

'You look after your wireless set, I'll look after my gun.'

Boden checked the sight once more; while it was true that the 2 cm Kwk 30 was only designed to fire armour piercing shot and not high explosive, he knew that he had to give Ebbing's infantry covering fire and that an accurately placed round could put the machine gun out of action.

Having re-laid the gun he gently pulled at the lanyard, and the turret rocked and filled with smoke, making a white luminous cloud against the electric light, as the ejected case fell back into the waiting basket behind Wundshammer's seat. For a moment Boden saw a red dot etched into the side of the cupola. The machine gun paused and started again. When Boden fired once more, the flash revealed a solitary assault pioneer, bent double and running towards the cupola slit, dropping to cover behind the overturned cement mixer, thirty metres from the machine gun position.

The French machine gunner must also have been aware of this new threat, for he changed targets and sparks flew as his fire crashed into the steel drum and cradle of the giant cement mixer. Boden held his fire when he saw a second assault pioneer drop a stick bomb into the aperture, but it rolled down the angled sill and exploded harmlessly in the deep concrete trench that protected the cupola.

Now Boden saw that the assault pioneer beside the cement mixer was carrying a harness with two cylinders on his back and was grasping a long nozzle attached to a hose connected to the cylinders. The machine gun suddenly increased its rate of fire desperately spraying the cement mixer. The grass on the ground above the archway had caught fire by this time and in its glow Boden could now see that the assault pioneer with the flame thrower was Ebbing.

There was a hiss as the gas pressure released by the oxidisation of the carbonic acid contained in the left hand cylinder spurted an initial oil jet into the cupola before Ebbing activated the ignition nozzle and with a roar a finger of flame sliced through the night, running along the ground and into the cupola.

Immediately there was a glow of light inside the strongpoint and a moving bundle of flames pushed its way through the slit, collapsing half way to the cement mixer. There was no more firing from the machine gun, and the smoke which accompanied the burning flameoil now clouded the approaches to the tunnel in an impenetrable curtain of darkness. But from the hill above the fort, Boden saw a triple red signal flare cascade out across the night sky. Then he ducked down into the Fighting Compartment as a 50 mm French Mortar shell exploded beside the cement mixer.

Someone was hammering on the starboard hull entry port.

'See who our visitor is, Seebohn.'

Seebohn pushed it open and Ebbing climbed in, his face black with oil.

He said briefly,

'We're going through the tunnel; but I shall be dropping

men off to stuff egg grenades and charges into the strong-points. Right now I'd rather be inside than out.'

'D'you want us to back you up?'

'That's up to you, and only if your driver can make it down that tunnel.'

'What d'you think, Wundshammer?'

'It should be all right.'

'How are you planning to get your men in, Leutnant?'

'With that.'

The light of another exploding mortar shell revealed the diesel locomotive standing beyond the switch attached to a line of flat trucks loaded with construction materials.

'Isn't this all a bit too good to be true?'

'That's the question I stopped asking after my first week of action in Spain. People who win battles accept risks and grab opportunities. You should know that anyway.'

Boden shrugged.

'If that's your decision, I'll go along with it.'

'Good, it only took ten men to take Fort Douaumont at Verdun. I've got eighty.'

Ebbing climbed up to the open turret hatch and looked around.

'The French have woken up at last and imagine they've surrounded us in a pocket. Not that I mind that too much. We'd soon find a way out if we really tried. They must have moved some infantry west of Les Cheniers, because they're letting off machine guns and mortars, but at that range the French are really lousy shots in the dark.'

Then Ebbing shouted out through the hatch,

'Werner!'

Half a minute later a pioneer Sergeant crouched down beside the tank.

'Yes?'

'How about fixing up that toy train to get our boys out of this mess?'

'So long as the fuel tank isn't empty anything's possible.'

'See you later then.'

'I'll give you a green light when we've got it fixed.'

Ebbing started to get out of the tank.

'Once we're through, I'll set up our light howitzer to cover the approach; we could use the train just for the pioneer equipment.'

The Sergeant must have worked fast for just then Boden saw the green signal light blink and Ebbing was gone.

Boden could tell quite easily that the mortaring was increasing in severity and that they were being enfiladed from the rear of the Fort. A whistle blew, and Boden saw assault pioneers piling onto the juddering diesel train.

'All right, Wundshammer, let's see if you can pass the advance driving test.'

The driver engaged first and the Mark 2 slowly moved across the courtyard towards the tunnel entrance. As they passed inside, it was clear that it would just be wide enough to accept the slowly revolving tracks.

Seebohn said,

'I like this detail less and less.'

Wundshammer said,

'Can't you keep quiet for once, Seebohn? I have a critical tolerance, and there is only half a metre to spare on either side, and I shall have to concentrate hard not to damage the track along which the infantry proposes to travel.'

Boden watched the circle of light from the fighting compartment running along the white glazed bricks of the tunnel roof, following the line of an electric power cable. He was suddenly aware of the overwhelming roar of the panzer's Maybach engine, echoing and re-echoing within the narrow confines of the tunnel.

'Seebohn, have you set the extractor fan on "maximum"? I don't want to suffocate.'

'Yes, but the set is dead.'

'That's hardly a surprise, now we're underground and you've let the aerial down.'

'It means we're cut off.'

'Yes, lots of things could happen; they could have even mined the roof.'

Seebohn looked tensely up out of the turret hatch towards the roof. In the distance Boden could make out a circle of light as big as a five mark piece held out at arm's length. He looked behind him to see that they were now being followed by the diesel.

Seebohn said,

'If they had an anti-tank gun trained on us from the far end, they could hardly miss.'

'There's no evidence that they have, is there? So I suggest you just sit tight and wait for it to happen.'

When they passed the first gallery Ebbing raised his arm, and two assault pioneers, one cradling a flame thrower, dived off, their boots stuffed with stick grenades.

Now the circle at the end of the tunnel was moving towards them and getting bigger. Glancing down Boden could see beads of sweat on the back of Wundshammer's neck as the panzer ground remorselessly on in second gear.

Boden said,

'You better not scratch the paintwork this time.'

'Begging to report, Herr Unteroffizier, I have not the least intention of doing so.' Wundshammer replied sarcastically. 'A gnat's whisker out in either direction and we'd probably never get out. Its a good job the MAN-Wilson steering's as good as it's cracked up to be.'

Another two assault pioneers dropped off at the next gallery.

Almost before Boden knew it the tunnel ahead had opened into a cavern forty metres square with the dusty, improbable look of a tramway terminal and the faintly incisive smell of new concrete. This must be the major crossroads of the complex where the principal galleries converged at the heart of the fort.

The narrow gauge railway ran off into the darkness of the large galleries to left and right and immediately ahead of them was a steel door shutter with embrasures on each side. As the panzer nosed into the dim lamplight Boden was almost deafened by the sound of machine gun fire reverberating below the low roof.

The train had stopped in the tunnel, and Boden could see that the assault pioneers had crouched down in the entrance. It would be certain death for any man to brave that withering fire.

Boden checked that the belt of 7.92 mm ammunition was correctly threaded through the M.G. 34 before aiming and reaching for the firing button on the traverse handle.

'Go forward, Wundshammer.'

As the panzer edged slowly forward Seebohn said,

'I hope they're not saving up any surprises for us.'

Wundshammer said,

'It looks like we're the surprise they hadn't allowed for. The assault pioneers would have been wiped out without us.'

By now the panzer was parallel to the embrasure slit, and Boden could hear the ringing staccato of the French machine gun's fire ricocheting harmlessly off the mantlet.

Boden fired a five second burst across the embrasure slit, and the machine gun fell silent. Then through the telephoto sight he saw three of Ebbing's men dashing between the panzer and the strongpoint, carrying a concentric charge. A Corporal waved to Boden to back off as the second assault pioneer, clambering up on his shoulders, thrust the charge deep into the embrasure and ignited the fuse.

Five seconds later there was a roar inside the strongpoint as pieces of concrete and smoke shot out from the slit. The roof shook and two wide cracks opened above the embrasure allowing rubble to pour through.

Boden climbed quickly out of the turret and made his way to the back of the panzer where Ebbing was crouching.

The Leutnant said,

'I'm certainly glad you came along.'

Boden smiled.

'That was a neat trick you pulled, but I doubt if the roof will stand much more of that kind of treatment. If you're thinking of fixing Hexogen charges to that steel door, the French'll be the only survivors.'

Ebbing gripped his arm.

'You've got us out of trouble once and you can do it again.'

'What? Batter it down?'

The Leutnant nodded.

'It's a tall order, I'll start off with armour piercing. That way it should only be the enemy that'll suffer.'

Boden ran back through the clouds of concrete dust to the starboard hatch and climbed inside.

'Wundshammer, position the panzer in front of the shutter door.'

As the driver moved the panzer into position Boden set his eye to the sight and adjusted the graticule, although there hardly seemed any point in taking accurate aim except for elevation, since, in his opinion, the weak points of the door would be at the top where it was masked by the concrete and masonry. The steel shutter door could be 100 mm thick, but it was extremely unlikely that the military engineer responsible for the blueprint had ever calculated that this inner complex would be subjected to fire at point blank range.

The sound of the first shot screamed back through Boden's ear drums in the confined space, and simultaneously a square metre of the door ahead glowed dull red. Boden aimed and fired again, his throat dry with cordite fumes, and this time the door seemed to rock back slightly as masonry began to fall from the keying above the entrance.

Seebohn shouted,

'The roof moved that time, you'll bury us all alive!'

'Balls, consider yourself buried alive anyway.'

The third hard shot vanished through the door, leaving a neat, round hole, edged with a ring of steel. Boden continued to fire off round after round in his own time until the surface was pitted like a pepper pot. Each time he fired more masonry slid away, until it began to form a barricade at the bottom of the door.

'All right, Wundshammer, that'll do, now it's your turn.'

'It'll dent the mudguards a bit.'

Boden could not take Wundshammer's worries seriously since he judged that the door was supported in a steel framework concealed behind the masonry, which would act as a roof support in any event. Wundshammer slipped the gear into first and ground over the points that marked the intersection of the narrow gauge railway at the tunnel junction. Then Boden was conscious of a violent shudder running through the hull as the panzer's nose armour pushed into the pock marked steel and Wundshammer slowly opened the throttle against the traction of the complaining tracks as the transmission whined while the Mark 2 ground into the door shutter. After a few seconds Boden could feel the walls shaking and a further rumble of falling masonry, this time on the far side of the door.

Now more masonry fell in front, bouncing off the track guard to reveal the steel frame that held the shutter door in two parallel channels and the massive chains that were used to raise and lower it.

'I'll try again, Wundshammer.'

The driver obediently brought the panzer back to its original position. Boden aimed at the top right corner of the frame and as he fired the Unteroffizier saw the door shift back half a metre as the chain links severed. Then he methodically fired at the opposite side until he had achieved the same result.

'You again, Wundshammer.'

The Rhinelander advanced the panzer to the door and this time the frame began to give against its weight, groaning and heaving and eventually parting from the concrete in which it had been set, so that it began to lean backwards. Now the panzer was attacking, not a vertical steel barrier but an inclined gradient and the four foot gap at the top was slowly increasing second by second.

Subjected to these forces, the 60 mm steel shutter was gradually toppling backwards. Boden realised that the weight of the Mark 2 panzer at its base was probably slowing down this process.

'Now back off, Wundshammer.'

'Thank you, right back into the fresh air so far as I am concerned.'

As the tank backed off, the base of the shutter levered up a narrow ridge along the concrete floor raising more dust clouds so that the fighting and driver's compartments were filled with a choking cloud of stone dust.

Now, as the Mark 2 panzer moved away under the shaking lights, Boden was aware that a group of assault pioneers, led by Ebbing, were already clambering up the heap of rubble towards the opening, through which they were tossing stick bombs.

'There goes the hero,' Seebohn said with a hint of envy.

'Our veteran hero; maybe you'd like to join him?'

'That sort of thing's not my job. What do we do now?'

'For a start you can go and shift that train somewhere else so that we can turn round and be all set to clear out.'

'Sod that,' Seebohn said with feeling.

'Oh, shut up Seebohn, you can't work the wireless in these conditions, so what else is there for you to do since you don't want to join the assault group?' He brushed the dust off his sleeve then, as Seebohn grumblingly made his exit, an assault pioneer banged on the panzer's armour.

'You Unteroffizier Boden? You're wanted.'

'Who by?'

'The Leutnant.'

'I thought we'd done our share.'

'I don't know anything about that. He's been hit. Wants to talk to you.'

The lights were still working the other side of the armour shutter, but Boden still stumbled over the bodies of two bereted and putteed Fortress troops and cursed.

Ebbing was propped up against the switchboard in the telephone exchange, where the French operators were all dead and the walls splashed with blood.

Ebbing lay back, his eyes closed. Boden thought he looked in a bad way; though quite how bad it was impossible to tell.

'What can I do? One of your men told me you'd been hit.'

'So I have, some French bastard got me through the chest.'

'Isn't there a medical orderly?'

'Right now I probably need an emergency unit, complete with surgeon, to do me much good.'

Ebbing's voice fell to a whisper as blood bubbled at his lips.

'Don't worry, we'll see you get out of here.'

'No doubt, but anyway that's not important.

The Leutnant gathered his remaining strength with an effort.

'Listen, there's one of my signallers working that switchboard.'

'So?' Boden asked gently, now aware that he was in the presence of approaching death. This time it was to some degree a personal matter, since he knew and respected Ebbing, even though it had only been for a short time.

'You can speak French can't you?'

'We all had to learn it at the Gymnasium.'

'Well, get on the switchboard and have my signaller call up the fort section by section; say you're on the staff and they're ordered to give up and go home. They shouldn't need much pushing.'

He pointed to the shelf beside the switchboard and the row of wine bottles with which it was littered.

'They were all half pissed when we broke in. That's why there was no serious opposition. This place is fifty metres underground but I don't suppose it's any different in the forward positions, probably a good deal worse in fact.'

'All right. Who am I supposed to be?'

Ebbing's brow wrinkled with effort as more blood bubbled.

'Say you're on General Corap's Staff, he commands the French Second Army. This was probably once his area.'

Ebbing shifted his position weakly.

'Before you go, I want to thank you and your men for what you did back there. Without you it would have been difficult. Not everyone would have gone along with my idea.'

'Think nothing of it.'

When Boden looked again Ebbing's hand had fallen slackly across the wound in his chest and there was nothing more that either of them could say. Nothing more, since Ebbing was now dead, so Boden pulled himself to his feet and picked up the phone.

* * *

All but one of the heavy 155 mm gun positions had obeyed General Corap's fictitious orders, and, loading double charges and attaching a length of signal cable to the firing lanyard, had withdrawn to a safe distance before destroying their guns. Then they had obediently proceeded to the Quartier General at the heart of the fort to await the promised evacuation.

However, instead of the waiting narrow gauge train ferry they had found smoke blackened German assault pioneers, who roughly disarmed them and smashed their weapons, in a grim mood as a result of losing their commander.

Boden watched them silently and it seemed to him that there had been some truth in Ebbing's final evaluation, since more than one or two were red faced and unsteady on their feet, and this was neither due to the shock of capture nor to running downstairs.

He picked up an unfamiliar gunmetal badge and looked at it curiously. Glancing up he found Wundshammer at his elbow, immaculate in his newly brushed uniform.

'On ne passeront pas? What the hell does that mean?'

'It means, Wundshammer, they won't get through. They being us.'

Wundshammer began to laugh. Boden felt he wanted to but couldn't, remembering the last person he had spoken to was Ebbing, who was now dead.

At last he said,

'Has the panzer been turned round?'

'Yes.'

'Then I think it's time to be off. I've had quite enough of special missions. If we're caught hanging about here, our next assignment will be to drive up the Eiffel Tower.'

'I know the feeling.'

'Where's Seebohn?'

Wundshammer said, 'Looking after the Mark 2.'

'Was that wise?'

'Don't worry, I removed the ignition key.'

'Oh well,' Boden said charitably, 'he's not so bad really, just new to the job.'

'He's not the only one. It just gets me how he's always sounding off about wanting to be a hero and being a party member on the one hand, and at the same time I can tell he can't wait to take off.'

This time Boden managed to laugh.

'We're all heroes, so we all deserve iron crosses.'

'That officer was certainly a candidate, but I hear he copped it.'

'Yes he did, worse luck.'

Wundshammer made no further comment; he didn't much care for officers in general since he knew it was impossible for him to argue with them, let alone question their orders. Besides, they often seemed to pick on him just because he liked living well. Boden knew how to handle officers and often acted as a buffer against their worst demands.

'Oh well, I expect they'll give him a gun carriage funeral.'

'So far as I'm concerned that's the least they can do. At least he behaved like a soldier. The French officers I've seen down here look more like male models.'

Boden lit an Eckstein.

'They're certainly not in the same class as the man on horseback.'

'He was fighting the wrong kind of war with the wrong kind of weapons.'

'You better talk to Seebohn about that, he's the expert military historian. I don't know anything about it.'

Boden picked up the note of irritation in Wundshammer's voice and said,

'Seebohn's all right when he's not being political, he's just got too much to live up to and he's not sure whether he can handle it.'

Wundshammer sighed.

'I wish I could believe you. All I want is for this to be over, and then it's back to civvy street for me, with or without decorations. I've got nothing to prove.'

'Then you're lucky. It must be rough to have a dead father who's been officially classified as a war hero. I think they even put up a statue so that no-one should forget about it.'

Wundshammer shook his head.

'No I'm sorry, if deep down underneath you're fundamentally a bastard I can't see what possible difference it can make.'

'Is that what you really think?'

'It's all a load of balls so far as I am concerned. The Führer can go and stuff himself so long as he keeps out of my hair. All I want is the steady job that's waiting for me at Neckar, without being paid danger money, and a nice little frau to cook my noodles the way I like them and darn any holes in my socks.'

'Nothing else? The trouble with you, Wundshammer, is that you have the wrong kind of ambition.'

When they got back to the panzer they found that Seebohn had picked up an abandoned MP38 from a dead assault pioneer and was threatening a demoralised group of French fortress troops with it.

Wundshammer said,

'See what I mean. That's all he's good for, taking it out on other people's prisoners.'

FT 17

ney drove west, crossing the Ardennes Canal idge beyond the burning ruins of Cheméry, ndary roads to try and catch up with the hich from the rumours they had picked up as now in the area of St Quentin.

ney turned off the secondary road that was ght mists to join Route Nationale 391 at

Nundshammer asked. 'North or south?'

to the west again as soon as we can, but cause that's in the direction of the Aisne to be the new French line. Besides, we involved in any more special operations.'

Wundshammer said,

'I'm all in favour of that, but I can't drive on like this forever. I shall start to fall asleep at the controls in a minute.'

'That's what they issued those Pervitin tablets for.'

'Oh yes, so that at least will cancel out the sleep problem. What about the food? There can't be much left in the larder.'

'There isn't, but don't worry, I'll think of something.'

Boden said to Seebohn,

'You'd better get the aerial up, now we're beginning to see where we're going. There's always a chance that we might re-establish contact.'

'What? On the move?'

'You know very well we can only stop if it's something important. I haven't given up our race to the seaside.'

Seebohn sullenly climbed out on to the track guard, clinging on precariously to pull up the two metre rod aerial from out of its channel, so that they might re-establish contact with the outside world. Then Boden heard him swearing over his throat mike.

'I can't, the bloody aerial's jammed.'

'Then unjam it, can't you?'

'Just tell that fat bastard Wundshammer to hold a steady speed or he'll throw me off.'

Wundshammer said,

'You're not registering yet another complaint are you Seebohn?'

What had happened was that the steel channel that had held the wireless rod had been buckled by the fall of masonry when they had made the attack inside the Maginot Fort. In the end Seebohn succeeded in removing the crowbar beside the engine grille and just managed to prise the channel open.

He replaced the crowbar and pivoted the rod aerial up to its vertical position. Then he tightened the wing nut.

After he had reported this to Boden, the Unteroffizier said,

'Now you'd better get through to the Herr Leutnant and tell him that the mission is accomplished.'

Although it was growing lighter, it seemed eerie to Boden to be driving across France away from the dawn, and he did not like it. After Ebbing's death he wanted the reassurance of Leutnant Von Dressen and the rest of the platoon. He had seen how Ebbing's men had reacted to the death of their commander, and now he knew that he would feel just as strongly if any of them were killed.

While it grew lighter, Boden could see that the surrounding countryside was dotted with scattered farms as the road began to climb towards a village called Bouvellemont. The red tiled houses sat clustered round a little hill with the church at the top.

'Anything on the radio, Seebohn?'

'Nothing very interesting. There's a lot of French traffic in code and I'm picking up 4th Army's Supply Net; they mostly seem to be putting in their daily requisitions for wurst, bread and gasoline. Our platoon must be way out of it, somewhere up in the north, they've got an eight hour start.'

'All except Richter,' Wundshammer commented.

Boden said,

'Richter could change track links left handed and blindfold at midnight in sixty seconds flat.'

Seebohn said,

'Some of the French stuff sounds quite close.'

'Of course it's close, we can't be more than ten kilometres from their front line. Have you any idea who or what they are?'

'D'you mean armour?'

'What else should we be worrying about?'

'It's impossible to say. Not all of their panzers are equipped with wireless; they even rely on flags. Besides, most of their wireless traffic has to be cleared at Vincennes, before they're allowed to get on with whatever it is they have in mind.'

The sun was already rising now and giving a whitish incandescence to the mists. The increasing light also revealed that, as they approached Bouvellemont, they were surrounded by the debris of war. There were craters in the adjacent fields and pieces of equipment littered the roadside, Adrian helmets, old fashioned rifles, knapsacks, greatcoats and gaiters.

'Just look at all that,' Wundshammer said.

'They're on the run before they've even started.' Then he added, 'I can't go on like this indefinitely, tell Seebohn to try and locate some French iron rations, frogs' legs and the like, that seems to be his line of country.'

Boden spoke over his shoulder to the wireless operator, 'Now's your chance to try out your basic training; jump off the panzer and go look for something nice to eat among that equipment. You can catch us up when we slow down to climb the hill ahead.'

Seebohn wasn't at all keen on this idea.

'Why's it got to be me?'

'Because you're not doing anything in particular, all right?'

Even Seebohn could see the logic of this and sullenly took the haversack Boden thrust at him.

Although the panzer was travelling at 30 kmh he made a reasonable landing and rolled into the ditch. As the Mark 2 drew away Boden could see him starting to rummage through the French equipment with gestures of disgust.

As the gradient increased, the Mark 2's speed dropped away to 16 and then to 8 kmh. Then Seebohn pulled himself in through the hullside port with a grin of triumph.

'There's plenty of tinned stuff.'

'Let's take a look at it.'

There were a dozen unmarked cans in the haversack painted chocolate brown and dark blue. Boden selected one and handed it to Seebohn.

'Grab the can opener and let's take a look inside.'

The tins didn't seem blown or otherwise unfit for human consumption.

Boden examined the contents, meat stew that smelled of nothing in particular.

'Get a spoon and pass Wundshammer his breakfast.'

Seebohn did so in silence while Boden examined the tins more closely, trying to decide which one to pick for himself. Suddenly he stopped. The chocolate brown tin in his hand was flaking and he could see that some words had once been lithographed onto the tinplate below. He carefully began to pick away the paint as he asked the driver,

'A good start to the day, eh, Wundshammer?'

'Hardly "haute cuisine" but passable, but I've got high standards. I can't wait to visit a Michelin five star restaurant. Ask Seebohn to open up another can.'

'Just hold on a minute.'

By this time Boden had succeeded in removing most of the paint that had covered the words underneath, but he stopped when he saw the date. That should be quite enough for Wundshammer.

'That's funny,' he called out. 'There's some printing under the paint on one of these cans.'

'Oh? Does it tell you what's inside?'

'Not exactly, but the date of manufacture seems to be March the third 1917.'

Boden could hear Wundshammer spluttering and choking with fury and the panzer lurched dangerously close to the ditch.

'I suppose that's Seebohn's idea of a joke!'

'No, he didn't know about that. But I think I can tell you what's inside too.'

'Oh you can, can you?' Wundshammer replied suspiciously.

'According to what the French Army have scratched on the tin it's "Monkey".'

Boden didn't stop laughing until they reached the first house in Bouvellemont and even Seebohn forced a smile. Wundshammer threw the spoon and the tin out of the driver's port in a rage and threatened to go sick the next chance he had.

* * *

This time as they entered the village one of the houses carried a giant advertisement for BYRRH and the Mark 2 panzer rocked across an involuntary barricade of dead high tension wires and telephone poles. For the first time Boden became aware of the clinging, sickly smell of death that came from the still smoking ruins and piles of rubble.

Seebohn began to look white again, and then with an effort seemed to recover.

'Let's get out of here.'

'What's the matter Seebohn, something bothering you? You'd better slow down, Wundshammer.'

'What's the big idea?'

'I've just had a feeling, that's all.'

'Well I don't want to slow down, I want to drive through as fast as I can. This place stinks.'

'I have the feeling that we are not alone.'

They were all of them quiet after that as Wundshammer nursed the panzer as gently as he could over the heaps of rubble, where flames still flickered from the exploded gas mains. A blue enamel street sign hanging from a shattered wall informed them that they had entered the Rue de la Republique. Once they crossed a final heap of rubble the way ahead seemed clearer.

Boden said,

'This will do. In beside the house on the right.'

Ahead, the Rue de la Republique turned sharply into the

Avenue Foch which in its turn ran into the south east corner of the Place Centrale. When Wundshammer had stopped, Boden beckoned to Seebohn and all three of them picked their way forward towards the Square through a back garden where curtains flapped at a shattered window and then past a burned out tobacconists with the red cigar sign still over the door, and lottery tickets for June still in the window. Boden took out his Walther 38.

Wundshammer said,

'The Bertas have been busy all right.'

Seebohn said to Boden,

'What's got into you?'

'Just a feeling. After all, we don't have any anti-tank guns to support us right now, which means according to the panzer textbook, we've no business to be alive.'

Boden clambered over a heap of collapsed and charred rafters.

'Just a feeling?' Seebohn said.

'Yes, come on.'

At that moment the Place Centrale came fully into view for the first time and when they saw what was there all of them froze with Seebohn nervously licking his lips.

The Place Centrale was a hundred and fifty metres wide, surrounded by shops and offices, some bomb shattered and others intact. The facade in front of them was dominated by the elaborate scrolls and moulding of the Crédit Lyonnais. This was not what had attracted their immediate attention, however. Between them and the far side of the Square, two solid lines of Renault FT 17 tanks were poised waiting.

Seebohn said,

'Jesus Christ, how are we ever going to get through that lot?'

The two lines of tanks stood menacingly, their shadows already lengthening away from the rising sun, their guns trained on the entrance to the Avenue Foch.

Wundshammer said,

'I've had all the surprises I need for one day. Let's clear out of here. Odds of twelve to one don't do anything for me.'

'Just hang on a minute,' Boden said.

A dog scampered across the pave and cocked its leg against the track of the nearest Char FT 17. Sideways on the tank looked like a cheap Japanese clockwork toy with its huge forward idler wheel and mushroom-like cupola above the tall fighting compartment. Having relieved itself, the dog sauntered off.

Boden said,

'Tell me, Wundshammer, would you let a dog do that to your tank?'

Wundshammer looked puzzled as though Boden had suddenly lost his wits. He shrugged.

A moment later Boden leapt to his feet and ran out into the Square.

'So! Wir hat bezahlen,
So! Wir hat viel geld,
So, Wir hat gepinke, pinke...'

'Pinke... pinke... pinke... pinke...' The walls shouted back but nothing else moved. The Unteroffizier walked up to the nearest Char FT17 and banged on the forward hatch.

'The war's over. You can come out now.'

Seebohn and Wundshammer glanced at each other agonisingly, convinced that at any moment Boden would drop to the ground, cut down by a hail of fire.

Suddenly Boden threw open the forward hatch and bellowed inside.

'Nobody there? What's happened to all the bloody French Army?'

Boden began to laugh with a force and volume neither of the two men had ever heard before. Then he sat down on the mudguard and scratched his initials, M.B., 6 Platoon, in the centre of the red Ace of Hearts, the Regimental symbol, that was painted on the turret.

Still uncertain, Wundshammer and Seebohn came up to join him.

'What went wrong here?' Seebohn asked with a serious expression, as though looking for somebody to blame.

'Nothing went wrong,' Boden said quietly. 'Except that the crews have buggered off. Don't you see, the whole Frog

Army's advancing backwards. I'll tell you something else – these tanks are vintage numbers out of a museum. They've only got machine guns for a start.'

The more he looked at them, the more Boden was reminded of Japanese toys with their crude green and brown camouflage and their tinplate armour.

'I can't believe it,' Seebohn said. 'They can have no honour.'

'Don't worry about things like that. See for yourself, look at the plate. They must have been keeping them in moth-balls.'

It was true; the oval brass plate riveted to the frontal armour read: Societe Anonyme Renault – Billancourt Seine. 1916.

Wundshammer kept on repeating,

'And they just buggered off. The bastards just buggered off.'

Boden said,

'That settles it. We better be on the move ourselves in case anyone comes back to pick up their scrap.'

As Wundshammer crossed the square in the Mark 2 panzer, threading his way between the lines of abandoned tanks, Boden said,

'Shall I prove to you there would have been no problem?'

'Fire away.'

Wundshammer halted the Mark 2.

Boden picked out a Renault fifty metres away, aiming at the Ace of Hearts on the turret and sending a hard shot round crashing through the brittle, unhardened 16 mm turret armour, tumbling it off its race, so that it stood rocking on its suspension like a helpless decapitated duck.

On his next shot Boden didn't bother to take aim properly and the round missed the second Char completely, slicing through the facade of the Crédit Lyonnais.

The impact of the shot shattered the elaborate scroll ironwork in front of the engraved and frosted glass and, passing inside beyond the Chief Cashier's desk, sliced into the front of the night safe, smashing the lock. Since the weight of the safe door gave it a tendency to open outwards the contents, some of them burning, were dispersed beyond the counter and, sucked out by the morning breeze, floated out across the Place Centrale.

Seebohn wanted to stop when he saw these large denomination Franc notes there for the taking.

Boden said,

'There's no point. You can't buy your life with bank notes. Those'll be worthless now anyway. Stick to your Deutsch Marks, you carry plenty of those.'

5 Chateau Auboncourt

When they came to Route Nationale 387 at La Bascule, it was soon evident that they had caught up with the transport columns moving up to supply the panzer armies. They had to halt at a crossroads and wait for a supply company of cart horses, drawing wagons filled with wicker shell cases, to plod by.

Wundshammer said,

'We'll never catch up at this rate.'

Boden said,

'Anyway they're heading south probably to Rethel or Rheims.'

'Champagne country. That's good news.'

'We're not going with them I'm afraid, I'd rather run the risk of bumping into the French down some country lane.'

Boden consulted the Michelin Map Seebohn had acquired at Flize.

'Once there's a gap in the horsedrawn artillery, we can cross over here and cut out a lot of kilometres by making for Fairsault. After that there are plenty of country roads running west. The rest of 6 Platoon will have to stop sometime.'

'Why should they?' Seebohn asked. 'There's no reason why they shouldn't go on until they hit the Channel.'

'Then we'll have to hurry to catch up with them, won't we?'

Then Wundshammer managed to cross the road before the next transport column came up.

'Anyway,' Boden said. 'I feel safer away from the feldgendarmerie, they're usually always Party men.'

They left the nodding horses behind them and the road began to take them through rolling but barren countryside. The sun rose higher over the fields where there was no evidence of war.

Now, in spite of the previous night and the imagined

confrontation with the French armour at Bouvellemont, they felt so exhilarated by the prospect of victory that their physical exhaustion was forgotten. Boden felt that they could keep on winning like this forever, there really seemed nothing to stop them, but he forced himself back into the reality of the present, as Wundshammer asked,

'Where do we go after this place Fairsault?'

'Laon, St Quentin, Arras. The shortest way.'

Wundshammer, driving with his visor open, had pulled down his goggles to keep out the dust.

'I don't know what all the panic's been about. There's very little evidence that the French Army ever existed except underground. They certainly haven't been this way at all.'

Seebohn replied,

'The Führer always said the French Army was a swindle and that there wasn't anything there; and yet the French were the architects of Versailles.'

Boden said,

'Well let's just be grateful that we haven't bumped into them since last night.'

Across the valley they were following, the chalky, whitish earth had been terraced. Vines trailed along these terraces on supporting wires in neat rows.

Wundshammer said,

'The wine'll be thin that they grow round here.'

'It could be Champagne,' Boden said, 'but maybe we're too far north.'

'You should know that, Wundshammer,' Seebohn said. 'It's a well known fact that all the Rhinelanders are champion boozers. I once went to a Stube at eight o'clock in the morning somewhere near Bonn, and you couldn't move for the people gulping down Hock, and most of them were half plastered.'

'Well Hock's better than that potato spirit the Baltic fishermen like so much. A Messerschmitt could take off on Schnapps, it's got so little character and refinement.'

The vineyards now stretched down to either side of the road so Boden could see the grapes had only just formed into dull little green berries much too immature to pick.

As the Mark 2 panzer came out of a re-entrant in the hillside, Boden noticed a clump of oak trees partially concealing the smoky blue and yellow roof slates and the white walls of a château. In the distance along the road ahead he could see the decaying lodge that marked the entrance. At the gate he saw a khaki figure and heard a distant rifle shot.

'What's going on?' Wundshammer asked.

'Here's your big chance, it sounds as if the Frogs have decided to stand and fight. Next turning left, Wundshammer, I'd never want to miss this opportunity.'

By the time they turned through the narrow entrance, bumping against the old brick wall, the khaki figure had vanished. Coming up the driveway Boden began to realise that something unusual was happening beyond the oak trees.

Thirty or more French soldiers were crowded menacingly around the house, but they did not seem to be aware of the sound of the panzer's engine. Pointing their rifles and shouting they were not interested in anything happening on the road.

Two women were standing with their backs to the main entrance, one of them holding a shot gun. Suddenly a French soldier stumbled forward clumsily, his rifle and bayonet at the charge, and lunged at the taller of the two women who had fair hair. She sidestepped at the last minute and he collapsed into the stone jardiniere beside the door.

It was then that Boden realised that the Frenchmen must be drunk, not simply deadened with alcohol, as the fortress troops had been, but violently and aggressively so.

A second private stumbled forward, looking even more incongruous because he had ripped the leather lining out of his Adrian helmet and now wore it to protect his head from the sun and to show anyone interested that he was no longer a combatant. Boden stopped the panzer and watched as this man dived at the dark haired woman, but as he almost grabbed her, the woman with fair hair pressed the trigger of the shot gun and the soldier collapsed with half his skull blasted away.

Others hit in the crowd behind began to scream, but those who were unhurt fumbled for their bayonets. The woman looked desperately to right and left, aware that she had only one more shot.

As the mob closed in on the women, Boden carefully aimed the MG 34 at the extremity of the crowd, his finger along the trigger mechanism.

Then, as if responding to a secret signal, the two women broke away and started to run towards an ornamental lake and the protection of the vines. The poilus followed them, shouting and stumbling and waving their rifles and bayonets, but the women were more desperate and quick footed, and soon they had a twenty metre lead. When they were clear of the field of fire, Boden pressed the trigger.

The first soldiers went down in a heap, those who followed on stumbling and tripping over them in bewilderment. Then one of them, not so drunk as the others, saw the panzer and threw away his rifle, slowly raising his hands above his head.

The rest crouched back from their dead and dying comrades against a red brick wall, obviously still not quite aware of what had happened.

Hearing the burst of machine gun fire the women had stopped and turned. The fair haired woman started to walk slowly back towards the panzer, holding her shot gun defensively.

Boden pointedly loosened the Walther in its holster and climbed out to meet her. When they were a few yards apart he gave her a military salute. Groping for the right words he started with an obvious question,

'What is happening here?'

The woman relaxed when she found that she was being spoken to in French. Boden could tell that she was still in shock, but with an effort of will she did not relieve her feelings by crying.

'They wanted the car. We told them it was impossible. There could be no petrol, not till tomorrow at least. But they didn't believe us. They said if they could not have the petrol they would rape us and shoot us. Isn't that right, Veronique?'

The second woman who was the same age as her companion was wearing a tailored suit and carrying a handbag.

'We were advised to leave today, but of course we couldn't without petrol for the car.'

'Who are they?'

'They wear Chasseur badges but they're really Les Joyeux, the Happy People – released ex-convicts.' Then she added bitterly, 'They're not the only ones that seem to have given up.'

Boden said,

'I expect there are many reasons, not all of them bad.'

The fair haired woman, who had an attractive, oval face, smiled her thanks at the Unteroffizier's tact.

'I can see that, otherwise you wouldn't have arrived with your tank just at the right moment.' She began to giggle hysterically. 'It is like a film.'

'Does this place belong to you?'

'I did own it. But now you've arrived as the occupying army, I just don't know any more. Both of us owe you a great deal, probably our lives.'

By now Seebohn, having climbed out of the panzer, had gone to inspect the prisoners.

'Seven are unhurt. Many of them appear to be drunk.'

The fair haired woman obviously understood the sense of Seebohn's remark for she turned to Boden and said,

'They've filled their canteens with Gniol, wood spirit, crude alcohol. It's supposed to improve their performance. Though I doubt it.' She looked over to Boden thoughtfully. 'Clearly German panzer crew don't need that kind of stimulus.'

'That doesn't make us total abstainers.'

'I'm glad to hear that. I'd like to give you some of our Champagne. Although the chateau isn't Grande Marque, the blenders sometimes use our grapes in the big wines.'

'I forgot to introduce myself. I am Micki Boden.'

'I am Charlotte. And this is Veronique. Call your friends over.'

'If you'll excuse me, first I must deal with Les Joyeux.'

Boden walked over to where the Frenchmen still lay huddled in terror in their ragged greatcoats and flapping puttees, clutching the waxed cloths with which they had been issued instead of haversacks.

'Who is the Corporal?'

A small red-headed man got up and ducked his head fearfully.

'Right, collect the rifles, bayonets and grenades and pile them in front of my tank.'

'Oui, mon Colonel.'

The Corporal beckoned to a second man who was on his feet and they began to pick up the 1895 issue rifles. It turned out that they had not been trusted with grenades.

'Collect up your rounds of ammunition separately, and when you've done that take each man's canteen and empty them over the rifles.'

Boden detected an undercurrent of protest and pointedly pulled out his Walther. The Corporal's assistant gathered the ammunition in one of the waxed cloths and handed it over to Seebohn, while the Corporal obediently poured out what was left of the Gniol over the weapons.

'Good. Now strike a match.'

In silence the Corporal groped in his greatcoat pocket.

'That's right, now let's have a bonfire.'

The spirit exploded with a 'whoosh' and the rifles were engulfed in flame.

Boden addressed the Corporal but made sure that the remaining French soldiers would hear what he had to say so that there wouldn't be any misunderstandings.

'Now you must dig graves for your comrades. Inside the tank there is a Sergeant who commands the machine gun. I have given him orders to shoot anyone who does not do exactly as he is ordered willingly and quickly. You must drag the bodies to the trees and dig a deep grave there. Deep, do you understand?'

'Oui, mon Colonel.'

'There you must bury your dead. Once you have done that, you are free to go. He will stay in the panzer for a long time. If he sees you coming back, he has orders to shoot.'

The Corporal blinked and frowned as though he hadn't heard the last bit properly.

'But Colonel, we are prisoners, your prisoners.'

'That is correct, and my orders are that after you have completed your duties here you must report to the nearest Assembly Point.'

'With you we shall be safe, mon Colonel. We have been looking everywhere for an Officer to whom we could surrender.'

'That is too bad. Although the war is over for you, it is not over for us. I cannot accept responsibility. You are lucky to have met me. After all, you are still alive.'

The Corporal was sufficiently intelligent to realise that he was beginning to tread on dangerous ground, taking all the circumstances into account.

'Oui, mon Colonel.'

'That is all. Do not waste any time. The Sergeant with the machine gun is not a patient man.'

Boden turned on his heel and walked over to the open door of the Chateau.

Although Charlotte was friendly enough, it was clear that Veronique was not quite sure what her attitude should be towards the panzer crew, but in the end her common sense prevailed and she invited Wundshammer to open another bottle of Champagne just after Boden had joined them in their drawing room.

'Well? And how did you manage that?' Wundshammer asked, pointing out of the window to where 'Les Joyeux' were furiously digging beyond the oak trees.

'With the help of the invisible man. I told them there was a German Sergeant in the turret with his finger on the trigger.'

Boden accepted the glass of Champagne that Charlotte smilingly offered him, while Veronique seemed equally pleased with Wundshammer's company, who, despite his unusual size, always seemed to be attractive to ladies. The only person who did not look happy was Seebohn.

'What's wrong, Seebohn?' Boden asked. 'Aren't you enjoying yourself?'

'The war is by no means over and yet you accept French hospitality. It does not seem correct to me, we should be on our way back to the Platoon.'

Charlotte asked,

'What is the matter with your friend? Doesn't he like our Champagne?'

Boden glanced over to her, admiring her regular bone structure and noticing for the first time that she kept her lips slightly parted as she listened, with an expression of intelligent interest. Although her hair was fair, her eyes were brown. Perhaps because of the wine and because she was reassured by Boden's presence, she seemed to have forgotten the unpleasant incident which had first thrown them together.

Boden answered her question with a shrug.

'He's just not used to the company of attractive ladies, any more than he can get used to the differences west of the Rhine. You have to realise that the only way of obtaining an exit visa in the Third Reich is by travelling abroad in uniform.'

Charlotte laughed,

'So I had noticed.'

Boden shook his head.

'No, you don't really understand; there's nothing anyone can do about it and live.'

'What are you talking about?' Seebohn asked irritably.

'Nothing, I was just explaining to Charlotte the logic behind your National Socialist attitude.'

'I still think we should be going.'

Wundshammer smiled and joined the conversation for a moment.

'This could be just as good as a week's leave in Paris if not better. You don't know what you might be missing. Anyway Seebohn, I'm sorry to have to dampen your devotion to duty, but there's been a technical hitch.'

'What kind of technical hitch?'

'The Mark 2's just about out of petrol. Maybe a litre or two, but that's about all.'

'Why the devil didn't you fill up at Bouvellemont?'

'Because I've too much respect for my engine to feed it rust and water. Anyway I didn't see you busy with a dipstick.'

Charlotte stood between the two men, first looking at one and then at the other as she tried to understand what the argument was all about.

Wundshammer went on,

'Now, if you were a good boy and really knew your job, we'd soon be out of this fix. Just tune your crystal set properly and call up the Supply Sergeant at Regiment and have him lay on a bowser.'

'I think I'll do just that.'

'Good luck to you then, Seebohn, I don't mind waiting here until Hell freezes over.' He looked speculatively to where Veronique was standing with her head on one side and smiling.

'Come to that, neither do I,' said Boden.

'Don't worry, we'll soon catch up with the Front, with or without your help,' Wundshammer called out as Seebohn walked angrily off. 'And I'll say goodbye to the ladies for you. Mind you leave the prisoners alone though, they've learned their lesson.'

'He was talking about petrol,' Charlotte said, wide eyed and eager to help. 'Now that is a problem that can be solved tomorrow morning. You see when my husband took the Lancia, he took all the petrol he could find in the garage, but he forgot that Lucien, our Remeur, has the keys for the emergency supply we put by to power the wine press.'

'What is a Remeur?' Boden asked.

'He turns the Champagne every day so that the sediment is deposited in the neck of the bottle. Oh yes, it is a very skilled job.'

'How do you know he will come tomorrow? If he didn't arrive today?'

'But he has been here today, only he leaves in the morning. He has a cottage a long way away from here; it was very difficult, especially with those soldiers.'

Charlotte seemed annoyed that Boden should question her competence in this way, so he said quickly,

'I must be sure about things like that. You do understand, don't you?'

'Oh yes. Lucien has been coming to the cellars at six o'clock every morning for the last sixty years, and I don't suppose that even the whole German Army would ever alter that. You see, when the petrol started to get short he locked away four hundred litres in the Inner Caves. There's enough for both of us I should think.'

Boden smiled.

'Then it's a race against time,' he said. 'Who'll get here first, the Regimental petrol bowser, or Lucien?'

Charlotte bit her lip and nodded slowly, a wisp of her fair hair drifting across her forehead.

'Either way, you're welcome to stay for as long as you like, although we shall be making our own way to Paris tomorrow. Nothing personal, but we know all about Occupations from what happened last time. Not all the personnel turn out to be as agreeable as you.'

'So you don't think the French Army will make a come-back?'

'I don't think anything, I just listen to the headlines on the news.'

'Well anyway,' Boden said, 'thanks for the offer. I think it's about two weeks since I've slept in a bed.'

Wundshammer said,

'That goes for me too.'

* * *

In spite of the agreeable company, Boden had difficulty in adjusting to the new situation, if only because it was totally unexpected. He had always thought of the Blitzkrieg as a combination of long advances punctuated by short, sharp panzer battles, rather different from the mopping up operations in Poland where the greatest threat had really come from the Soviets.

Now, standing in the panelled drawing room of this

sixteenth century château, he was tasting the fruits of victory, even though the campaign had only just begun. He couldn't get over the welcome they had had from the French women. There was no evidence of the legacy of past bitterness and hatred.

Nevertheless he still found it hard to understand Charlotte's attitude; one minute shooting a French soldier and the next entertaining the enemy. When he thought about it he realised that he had expected nothing more than cold and reluctant thanks for saving their lives.

From the reception they had had, it was hard not to believe that Charlotte and her friend had wanted them to stay and at the same time they were driving south the next morning. In the end he gave it up as hopelcss, unable to assess these conflicting factors. Maybe every victim does attract an attacker and he wondered what would emerge from their relationship in the end. Perhaps Charlotte might consider that a few glasses of Champagne and a smile would be more than adequate compensation.

He found that Charlotte was smiling speculatively at his empty glass.

'Some more Champagne?'

'No thanks.'

Then she added unexpectedly,

'You've travelled a long way in the last few days. I expect you would appreciate a bath.'

Boden had deliberately suppressed this desire for some days now, although there was always the possibility of coming across a Wehrmacht Mobile Shower Unit. As he knew from Poland, it was impossible to tell when the bath units or mail were going to arrive although they inevitably did in the end. Given the choice, he would have a bath rather than a meal every time.

'Yes, I would very much.'

'Good, then that's simple.' She paused. 'By the way, Micki doesn't sound a very German name to me.'

'And the French haven't cornered a monopoly in Charlotte.'

'Oh yes, you're right, of course. I just wondered. Go

upstairs whenever you feel like it. The bathroom's down the corridor, the second door on the left. Later on we'll have dinner.'

'Haven't you done enough as it is?'

'I don't think so, anyway that's Veronique's idea, she's afraid that the soldier who drives your panzer might be undernourished.'

Boden smiled and said,

'It looks like we're starting a new chapter in Franco-German relations.'

As he went out into the hall to go upstairs, Boden was impressed, in spite of himself, by the feeling of age and luxury that surrounded him. Everything was so new in Germany these days, and for most people it was fashionable to be modern especially since this identified them with the Party that claimed to be sweeping aside the clutter of the past.

Most of the things that were modern in Germany had appeared in the thirties, like the Mark 2 Panzer, although even better weapons were in the pipeline. The FT 17 with its machine gun and top speed cross country of 2.5 km should have gone to the scrap heap long ago.

Boden climbed the marble staircase with its wrought iron banisters to the first floor. When he came to the door leading to the bathroom he started to unbutton his uniform which he had now worn for ninety-six hours, ever since the Regiment moved from Trier. However the door led not to a bathroom but an entire bedroom suite complete with two dressing rooms. Thinking no more about it he turned on the old fashioned bath taps before carefully removing his black uniform jacket and trousers, and hanging them on the hangers he found in the wardrobe.

The bath was deep and took some time to fill, and while he was waiting he glanced out of the window, but could see no signs of 'Les Joyeux' except for a mound of freshly dug earth behind the oak trees. When he looked down onto the gravel drive in front of the house he could see Seebohn's head from time to time at the turret hatch while he fiddled about with the aerial.

As he was in the bath he thought he heard the bedroom

door open and close but soon forgot it as he reconsidered the last thirty six hours. For once Hitler had been right; when France had been put in its place and the injustices of Versailles finally corrected as they had been since the Saar Plebiscite, the rest of Europe would settle down, and the whole wretched and bloody charade of nineteenth century European diplomacy thrown out of the window for good. Europe could still be the continent of the future, despite its past; these days nobody seemed interested in colonies, except the British.

Stepping out of the bath as red as a lobster Boden realised that he had forgotten a towel, although there were plenty in a pile in the cupboard next to where he had hung up his uniform.

Dripping on the Chinese carpet and shivering slightly, Boden crossed the bedroom to reach the dressing room, and stopped.

Charlotte was sitting on the edge of the bed in her slip and stockings, brushing her fair hair in a slow, regular rhythm. If she had noticed him, she showed no sign of it, although she could have hardly failed to see him. Boden felt a great wave of desire as he watched her, as though she represented a reward for the days of hard campaigning. Nevertheless he still felt embarrassed because he had no towel.

The truth was that he had never been able to take a girl to his room back home in Gottingen. The sexual adventures that he had indulged in before and during Army service had had to be mostly in the woods or cinema.

Charlotte got up and moved to the dressing table to pick up a Coty hand spray, her breasts tilting under her slip. She returned to her original position on the bed, sitting in a way that was somehow vaguely improper, possibly because it unduly emphasised the invitation of her thighs.

Boden went off to the cupboard to collect a towel.

When he crossed the bedroom again, Charlotte had lit a cigarette, which although it could hardly be described as an immodest action, notched up the sexual tension still further. To Boden her every movement was now a provocative invitation.

She said, without looking up,

'Somebody has to collect the prize I suppose.'

'What about your husband?'

'Oh yes. What about him? He talks a great deal and is quite inoffensively ineffective except over things like doing a bunk and leaving me to face the consequences, which I am now doing entirely of my own free will.'

In the silence that followed Charlotte crossed her legs.

'I hope you like me, we foreigners have heard that there's a lot of homosexuality in the Party and that women aren't fashionable any more. I've even read that the Führer has leanings in that direction. However, considering the lack of sex appeal displayed by most German women, I don't suppose anyone can be blamed for that. Oh yes, but I see where your interests lie.'

Boden was conscious of the increasing tension at his loins which, by this time, had become obvious even under the towel.

'Clearly I won't have to teach you anything about the politics of sex.'

Boden moved towards her and, dropping the towel, slid his penis inside the leg of her lingerie so forcefully that the material tore at the crutch.

She raised her legs as he penetrated her, giving out a long, ecstatic sigh and stretching her arms across the bed, her lips slightly parted and her eyes shut.

Moving inside her, Boden felt the tensions of the last twenty four hours relax.

Charlotte said,

'Oh yes. That is what is so nice about you Germans, you are so forceful, but after a little time that becomes tedious because, chéri, there is no substitute for... technique... and imagination.'

Suddenly she had twisted out from under him and stood at the far side of the bed. She pulled up her slip to show how her clothes had been torn.

'Now look what you've done. It was really quite unnecessary. I would have undressed for you if you'd asked me. I really don't know what you take me for with your violent bedroom manners. I'm not some little fraulein out of a Bier Keller who only feels she's wanted when she's been given a black eye. Just because you've been given a little aperitif, that doesn't mean you can smash up the cellar.'

Boden lay on the bed and glared at her.

'What the hell else do you want? All this was your idea. We've never set eyes on each other before this, and we're not likely to again.'

'Then why don't we give each other something worth remembering? Fighting can't be much fun; rather squalid, I should think.'

With a sudden movement, Boden gripped her wrist and pulled her back onto the bed. As she struggled to get out of his grip the nails of her right hand dug into his chest leaving a long and bloody trail. Now there couldn't be any question about it, she really did want to get free.

'You seem to forget that your country is at war with mine.'

Then suddenly she went limp and Boden relaxed his grip slightly, trying to work it out.

'Let me go.'

'All right if that's what you want.'

'See – now you have laddered my expensive stockings. Pure silk.'

She ran her fingers lightly across her thigh. Then she laughed.

'You are clumsy, and I really don't know why that should be.'

In a flash she was at the bedroom door and turning the key in the lock. But Boden was too fast for her and slammed her wrist against the wood until she dropped it. Charlotte screamed with surprise, pain and fright. At the same time, Boden scooped his penis into her thighs until she began to sink down on him, her body relaxed and her eyelids drooping. Finally giving way to him, her breasts fell out of her torn slip and she sighed and heaved to his rhythm. When she reached her climax her thighs contracted so violently that she almost threw him off.

Afterwards she sat on the blue Chinese carpet, putting back her hair. She did not say anything as Boden washed and got dressed, not quite sure of her reaction. As he was about to leave she looked up at him, following him with her eyes as he went towards the door.

'Oh yes, now you must see how a little dash of pepper always improves the dish.'

Boden smiled and kissed her on the forehead as he went out.

* * *

By the following morning, Seebohn, who had spent most of the night vainly attempting to contact Regimental H.Q., was in an evil mood. His temper was not improved by the sudden appearance of Lucien as predicted on the dot at six o'clock. Seeing Seebohn at work through the starboard hull port, Lucien stopped and looked owlishly through the panzer.

'Hey Fritz, you can have your petrol.'

'Where is it?'

'In the cellars. The Countess said you can have it, so you can have it.'

Seebohn looked at the strange little old brown faced man in his black beret, blue overalls and espadrilles. Suddenly Lucien spat on the ground beside the panzer track.

Seebohn shouted,

'Filthy swine! You French are all the same. You have no sense of order!'

In fact neither could understand enough of the other's language to communicate meaningfully, but only sufficient to catch the general drift. Lucien had the advantage of having played this game of noncommunication before and, speaking as though he was making some important announcement which would be of special interest to Seebohn, he said,

'I don't have to kiss your fat, pig-like Boche arse just because the Countess says so, and by some lucky fluke you appear to be winning the war because we are commanded by incompetents!'

6 Somua 35 and Char B

At 7.15 a.m. Seebohn finally got through to the Leutnant. The signal was weak, which could only mean that if he was transmitting direct he was at least 35 kilometres away, although the signal might be relayed.

'The Regiment has hit St Quentin. Where are you?' Von Dressen asked Boden.

'Somewhere north of Rethel. A place called Auboncourt.'

'Any problems?'

'One or two, but none that we couldn't handle.'

Boden glanced over to Wundshammer, who was smiling. The Leutnant's voice rose and then faded away.

'I want you to rendezvous with me at Arras, which looks like being our next objective, but first there's something brewing near Montcornet. An Arado reconnaissance plane has spotted French heavies moving across the Aisne, but we want to know more before we launch an air strike with the Bertas.'

Boden felt the same twinge of alarm he had felt before in the pit of his stomach.

'Heavies?'

His rising fears could not totally erase his memories of Charlotte, since every time he moved he was reminded of her body's perfume.

'Yes, Boden, heavies and mediums. Not horses and history book infantry this time, it looks like being the real thing. Second Army have put out a call for every available panzer. It's quite clear that the French are intending to punch through our L. of C.'

'Where do you want us to go, Herr Leutnant?'

'Contact 201st Regiment outside Thuringy. They'll tell you what to do.'

When the Leutnant had signed off, Seebohn said,

'If only Wundshammer hadn't scraped the General's mudguards we wouldn't keep on getting in these messes.'

Boden said,

'I'm surprised you feel like that about it, Seebohn, I always thought you wanted to finish off the war single handed. Now you've got the chance you suddenly lose interest.'

'I like being in a team. I can't stand being shunted about at everyone's beck and call. It's not what I expected.'

Boden said,

'This campaign is not what anyone expected.'

* * *

Coming up to Thuringy, the sun had thrown up a heat haze that made the poplars dance in the middle distance.

Wundshammer said,

'There's a panzer over there in the next field. Looks like something nasty's happened to it.'

Seebohn said confidently,

'It's bound to be French.'

The short 50 mm gun of the Mark 3 panzer was depressed towards the ground, and as they approached they could see that the hull was blackened by fire.

'Christ,' said Wundshammer. 'It's one of ours and the sort that has double our armour.'

Passing the tank, they saw the body of a black uniformed panzer crewman face down in the scorched grass surrounding the tank. His tunic had been burned off his back and all that remained was a tissue of singed fabric along the sides. His back was a red raw burn and his left arm and shoulder were missing. Then Boden noticed that his severed forearm was wedged between the line of spare track links below the turret, and fought to regain his self control as the panzer disappeared behind them.

After that they came to the road and a sign marked '201st Regiment', and Boden ordered Wundshammer to stop as they came to a cluster of roofless, burned out farm buildings.

Boden swallowed and said,

'After that latest reminder I intend to rely on speed. I'll choose the ground as carefully as I can, but if that's what they can do to one of our mediums, I'm certainly not going to present them with an easy target.'

Boden stopped the panzer and walked across to where a Hauptsturmfuhrer was sitting beside a farm gate, kicking his feet against the wall while examining the hills ahead through field glasses. He wore field grey and a soft peaked field cap with the SS skull and crossbones.

After saluting, the Unteroffizier said,

'I've been ordered to report to 201st Regiment, Herr Hauptsturmfuhrer.'

At first the S.S. Officer took no notice of him.

Finally he said,

'They're not here any more.'

After a few moments Boden asked,

'Perhaps you have some suggestions?'

The Hauptsturmfuhrer glanced at the Mark 2 panzer.

'So those are all the reinforcements we're getting. Well, that's just fine. What kept you?'

'We had to draw petrol.'

'I see. For your information I've sent out three 35ts on reconnaissance, and two of them have run foul of the reception committee.'

'I don't understand you, Herr Hauptsturmfuhrer.'

'Over there, at eleven o'clock.'

Boden raised his glasses to a smudge of smoke rising above a fold in the hillside two kilometres away where a Skoda panzer was still burning.

'What went wrong, Herr Hauptsturmfuhrer?'

'They all made off down this lane and the flea brains didn't get across to the cover of the woods for some reason. I've seen dozens of French Chars moving about on the ridge at one time or another, there's probably a whole French Panzer Regiment somewhere up there.'

'And what are we supposed to do?'

'Take a look and see whether or not it's just my over-heated imagination. You're also in support of the Army boot boys, the ones you can't find. They're stuck somewhere on the ridge behind those burning panzers. If you hit trouble you can't handle, the Stukas are there to help you; they're tank busting experts by now.'

'After that what happens?'

'Cross the Aisne, for all I care, or better still don't switch off until you get to Paris.'

'D'you know what stopped our panzers, Herr Hauptsturmfuhrer?'

'I told you, what seemed to be some fairly impressive armour, though I suppose it could have been a French SA 37 on the loose. Now run along and let me watch you earn a Ritterkreuz.'

'Yes, Herr Hauptsturmfuhrer.'

Boden saluted and marched off, glancing back enviously at the Officer at his secure observation post. The officer called out,

'Don't worry, I won't go away. I might even be here if you make it back. O.K. Dismiss.'

On his way to the Mark 2 panzer Boden tried to control his anger. Climbing in through the turret he said tightly,

'All right, Wundshammer, follow the track until I tell you to stop.'

'Just what's eating you, then?'

'That patronising SS swine. We're just bait on the hook so far as he's concerned, so the French'll be on their toes while the mediums move round through the back door. At least that's what I suspect.'

Boden decided that there was little point in passing on the bad news about the burning Skodas since the tension inside the turret was already sufficiently high.

Seebohn said,

'Whatever you say I wouldn't mind being SS.'

Boden grunted.

'Why don't you join, then? Are you racially impure or something?'

Seebohn saw that Boden was upset and said diplomatically,

'No, my fallen arches let me down.'

Wundshammer said,

'If you've got flat feet, a mechanised arm is the logical outfit to join, but why pick on us?'

When they got to the end of the track, Wundshammer crashed through the farm gate that barred the way.

Boden said,

'Keep your eyes open for the hikers. They must be around somewhere.'

Seebohn said,

'You'd better drive really carefully for a change.'

Now Boden could see that some good cover would be provided by the copses ahead, but the rolling, smooth hill-side to the east where the burning panzers lay was naked and unbroken except for a stream bed.

'Where to for the first jump?' Wundshammer asked.

'The hill with the pines on it.'

Seebohn suddenly said,

'I never believed that war could be like this – the country-side seems so peaceful.'

'Just hope that it stays that way,' Boden said. 'Anything could happen once we're in those woods.'

Having passed through the farm, they picked up a track that ran in the direction of the hill, crossing a field littered with the inflated bodies of dead cows. The stink of corruption hung heavily in the heat haze. A cow with a distended udder had been trapped by its forelegs in the wire fence. Its agonised bellowing was suddenly interrupted by the sound of machine gun fire echoing out hollowly across the flat and empty skyline ahead.

'Slow down, Wundshammer,' Boden ordered.

Beyond the pines the smooth, long hillside, broken by the watercourse, lay to the left, and to the east and right the hillside merged with a fir plantation stretching away as far as Boden could see.

The Unteroffizier said,

'There's only one way up so far as I'm concerned, and that's not the way the others went. What d'you think, Wundshammer?'

'Don't ask me. When God built Koblenz he put it at the junction of the Rhine and Mosel because it seemed the only thing to do. We are in his hands.'

'Yes,' said Boden, 'and the obvious thing for any anti-tank outfit would be to defilade that stream bed. That's why I'm going up through the wood.'

As the panzer advanced, Seebohn asked,

'Shall I keep the wireless link open?'

'Isn't there a special channel reserved for the Stuka frequency?'

'Nobody tells me anything.'

'Well do something about it, will you? I thought even you would have realised that's the only real protection we've got where we're going.'

Boden began to try and work out how it was that the other three panzers had come to grief so obviously. It all seemed so badly organised. Three in a row, one after the other, the sort of operation he would have expected from the French. To send out a forlorn hope three times in succession to be destroyed was almost beyond belief. More worrying still was the lack of any positive intervention on the part of the Luftwaffe.

Ahead was the fir plantation, and now Boden could see that a crudely stencilled plate had been nailed to each tree at twenty metre intervals. The message on each plate was simple and direct; MINES – DANGER DE MORT, below a skull and crossbones. Boden saw panzer tracks running parallel with the edge of the wood away from the warning signs.

At the same time Wundshammer said,

'Here are the hikers.'

Boden concentrated on the ground ahead.

'There's nothing I can put my finger on.'

'They're there all right, they've put on quite a show in the way of camouflage.'

'You'll have to be careful then, won't you?'

'I will, don't worry about that.'

'You better make for that fir plantation.'

Wundshammer moved uneasily, 'You've seen what it says?'

'I know. It says there's a minefield.'

Wundshammer moved nervously to the edge of the wood.

'Looking for cover or something?' Wundshammer asked.

'Right the way inside.'

Wundshammer said,

'I hope we'll be alone once we're through the mines.'

Boden considered the driver's remark for a moment, and then suddenly realised that he was guilty of a mistake. In his mind he automatically equated 'the front' with the ridge ahead, simply because that was where the panzers lay smouldering and the Hauptsturmfuhrer had told him so. There was no reason to draw a line across the countryside and expect to be free from attack until that line was reached. That really was the Maginot Line mentality in action.

That led him to something else. The French obviously wanted them to believe that the front lay along the edge of the wood because of the warnings against mines. It would, however, be much better to mine the wood and then let the enemy find that out in their own time. The only conclusion he could reach was that the minefield did not exist and the whole thing was a bluff to deter German armour and infantry from entering the wood. It clearly had had the desired effect so far as the commanders of the Skoda 35ts were concerned.

Then Boden said,

'All right, Wundshammer, I'll let you off for the moment, just cruise along by the cover. The next jump will be the ruined buildings over there to the west. Follow the stone wall round to those beech trees. I'm not taking short cuts over open ground at this stage.'

The panzer's tracks began to scoop up dustclouds as they followed the track beside the wood, where there were still warnings of mines.

'Get off onto the field.'

Wundshammer moved along the edge of the field planted with early maize. Boden focused his glasses on the ridge as he thought he caught sight of steadily moving hulls.

'Just keep going. Seebohn, have you got through to the Stuka Controller?'

'Yes, I have the frequency.'

'And have you given him the grid reference?'

'No. Which targets do you want me to identify?'

'The ruined cottage we're making for, the stream down

the hillside to the south east, and the southern edge of this wood along the ridge.'

Boden paused for a moment as he wondered whether the destruction of the German armour could have been caused by a mistake over target references. If the sequence of figures was either inadvertently reversed or inaccurate, the consequence might be some futile attack on an imaginary target miles off the map. It was unlikely, but no more unlikely than what had happened. It was also obvious that the tank commanders before him had believed the warnings against mines.

Boden listened to Seebohn checking the references off the grid map.

'They've just acknowledged; the strike codes are "Blue" for the ruined buildings ahead, "Red" for the stream and "Yellow" for the wood. They've told me there's a Stuka Circus south of Laon. All we've got to do is press the button and they'll give us what we want, where we want it.'

'Well, I see no sign of them,' Boden said tightly, straining his eyes into the empty, cloudless sky.

As the panzer moved slowly up to the ruined cottage, Boden at last saw a group of assault troops in the shadows. They seemed nervous to Boden, quite different from the confident infantry that they had seen marching along the road before the Meuse Crossing.

The Officer, who was not wearing insignia, pushed his way through the men.

'201st Regiment?' Boden asked.

The Officer nodded.

'I'm glad you came this way.'

'Why? Didn't the others?'

'They all took a short cut to the next world along the wood and then up the side of that hill we've been trying to infiltrate since yesterday.'

'What about the wood?'

'It's not mined so far as our patrols can make out, but we think it could be registered for their heavy artillery, so for the moment we're keeping outside and on the edge. We've got the feeling that we've hit real opposition for the first time.'

'French armour?'

'Right. These are impressive. I've got one or two forward outposts on the edge of the ridge, but as soon as the French heavies put in an appearance, the balloon really goes up.'

The young Leutnant was clearly worried by his lack of progress. Then he went on,

'I lost six men moving up the 35 mm anti-tank, and even when we got it into position they were overrun almost at once, the solid shot simply bounced off the glacis plates of the French armour.'

Boden's mouth went dry as he said,

'I'm not here to act out David and Goliath; so far as I'm concerned we're target spotting for the Stukas.'

The young Leutnant lit up an Eckstein that one of his men offered him.

'That's what the others were supposed to do, too. If the French break through here there's nothing much to stop them except anti-tank grenades. Once they've got past us they could slice through Twelve Army's southern pincer as far as the Belgian frontier. That could make a real field day with most of the forward elements cut off in a cauldron.'

'What about their infantry? From what we've seen of it, it doesn't rate.'

'We've not met any. I'd be happy enough to take them on, it's their armour that puts the wind up me.'

Boden said,

'All right, I'll see just what is up there.'

'I'll send a couple of men with you, they've been out in that wood often enough and they'll show you the way they use. Buchser, Lansdorff, fall out.'

When Boden climbed back into the turret and the panzer moved forward, the horizon ridge now seemed ten times higher, like a suddenly built up wall.

Wundshammer said,

'I don't like this. I always believe warning signs. I didn't volunteer because I wanted to be a hero, only for the extra meat ration.'

Boden said,

'We're going in because it's the safest place. You'd agree

if you'd seen what happened to the Skodas. Anyway, nobody's volunteered for anything. We all had our call up papers through the letterbox.'

'But Seebohn's a volunteer. Seebohn doesn't mind dying, he can't wait to get to Valhalla and be rated a big hero.'

Boden said,

'Well, we're stuck with it one way or another, so let's get it over and done with.' He glanced forward to check the progress of the two infantrymen who were leading. In any case Buchser had told Wundshammer,

'Take the track on the left and follow it right the way to the top.'

The track zig-zagged in and out of the woods where Red Admirals fluttered in the patches of sunlight.

Wundshammer ground up the chalky clay track in bottom gear until they came to a clearing where the trees had been cut down, and there the track ended. Boden told Wundshammer to switch off the engine and waited for the two assault troops to lope back to the panzer. There was no sound except for the rustle of the wind through the branches and the buzzing of flies which descended in a cloud over the open turret once the panzer had come to a halt.

Buchser stopped and checked his helmet camouflage, replacing some twisted maize leaves with sprigs of pine to break up the silhouette, then he carefully smeared his face and hands with mud from beside a tree stump.

He stood up and said to Boden,

'Right here, we're maybe fifty metres from the outside of the wood. The other panzers went up in the open as you know.'

'Yes, and I'm also acutely aware of what happened to them. Where's the ridge?'

'About five hundred metres further up, at least that's where it really starts, inside the wood.'

Suddenly Boden realised that they were talking to each other in whispers as though they were trespassing.

Lansdorff said,

'We'll go and take a look-see.'

Boden glanced at the wall of trees ahead of them. They

were not mature and clearly would not make a formidable obstacle.

'I shouldn't bother. We'll move on.'

As he spoke he became aware of a distant crashing and the throb of engines two hundred metres in front of them. Buchser and Lansdorff exchanged uneasy glances.

'That sounds like their heavies all right.'

'They've got big enough engines by the sound of it, as much guts as our Mark 4 panzers.'

'They're not using them in ones and twos, either.'

Lansdorff said,

'If there's any danger of there being a tank duel, I'd rather watch it at a safe distance.'

Boden felt his stomach tighten once more.

'I can't say I blame you.'

The woods ahead seemed a turmoil of snapping tree trunks and waving branches, as though a slow motion hurricane was passing through. When Boden looked again the two infantrymen had vanished into the shadows of the larger trees.

Boden said to Wundshammer,

'All right, switch on and move off.'

Wundshammer rolled his eyes.

'Joking apart, this is crazy. We'll never stand a chance and you know it.'

'Not at all, we stand the best chance in the wood. That way we can penetrate their flank and really see what's going on.'

'Penetrate their flank?'

Seebohn said,

'Shouldn't I call up the Stukas?'

'Not until we can give them the best possible target, otherwise we'd be wasting everyone's time.'

Wundshammer grimaced.

'I never thought of myself as a woodcutter before.'

'Don't worry, there's a first time for everything. Now start moving south west.'

The panzer slowly edged forward across the tree stumps and out of the clearing. At first Wundshammer tried to avoid the trees, but when they became thicker he had no alternative but to crash into them.

After a hundred metres the trees thinned out as they came to a through lane, carved out of the wood by the French armour. Trees were splintered and shattered along a ten metre wide corridor.

'Get over and make it fast, Wundshammer.'

But when they came to the lip of the track that the French tanks had carved out, the Mark 2 panzer became entangled with the branches of a fifteen foot fir tree, so that its solid trunk, having been caught between the third elliptical spring and a starboard upper return wheel, began to jam the upper track against its guard, as a prelude to prising it off the drive wheel. As a result the panzer began to twist right.

'For Christ's sake move it!' Boden shouted.

Wundshammer said,

'I'm not a miracle worker. I'll have to reverse.'

As the engine idled for a moment in neutral, Boden could hear the sound of an approaching panzer.

Wundshammer backed away from the panzer trail and Boden could now tell by the engine note that they were free of the obstruction. Then an olive and apple-green camouflaged shadow rumbled out of the trees to the left. Almost three metres high, it seemed to Boden a menacing steel pyramid, the apex topped by the Command cupola dome. The forward turret faces carried the red, white and blue identification target of the French Army on each side of the stubby 47 mm gun. The track plates, shiny with constant use, crunched into debris of shattered tree stumps at the edge of the trail.

At the approach of the Somua S35, Boden had traversed the turret, bringing his 2 cm kwk 30 to bear a metre and a half above ground level to the right, so that he could defilade the Somua as it passed through his gun sight. This meant that, provided they remained undetected, there would be time to fire two shots before the French Commander could stop, turn and lay his gun. Because of the French armour's thickness, Boden would have to wait until the last possible moment before he opened fire. It was impossible to tell what target the Mark 2 panzer made, only partially camouflaged by the broken trees at the side of the track, but with surprise on their side they could get away with it.

Seebohn crouched down uneasily in the wireless operator's seat as Boden watched the approach of the French panzer through the rear visor.

'Why the hell don't you fire?'

'Shut up, can't you, and leave it to me.'

Wundshammer began to hum, not loudly but audibly enough to relieve his feelings in the black cloud of fear that had suddenly built up inside the panzer.

Seebohn said,

'Why doesn't he make it the Horst Wessel song?'

'Shut up,' Boden said again. 'I don't want songs about dead heroes. I'm coming out of this in one piece.'

Boden now watched the Somua coldly, waiting for it to enter his field of fire. His first shot had to be decisive. He ordered himself not to move the Zeiss sight until he could read the number plate, but even when he could make out the word SOMUA above the miniature tricolour and five figure registration number he waited. His left hand stretched out across the fighting compartment to the gun support, his mouth a tight, thin line, as his senses strained for any change in the Somua's engine note or direction which might indicate that they had been discovered. Through the rear visor, he could see light and shade from the trees above, dancing over the engine compartment behind him.

As the noise of the French Char's engine and the clatter of its tracks increased, Boden found that his hand was shaking. He began to wonder if he had depressed the gun too far and might miss the target altogether.

Then he found himself staring into the French driver's raised visor. Inside he could see the driver in his crash helmet with its leather rim band; he wore a black Gallic moustache, like a film star, staring blindly past Boden.

Boden now moved to the front of the turret, pressing his eye to the Zeiss sight to view the dreamlike telescopic image that began as a camouflage blur and became in succession the bulging outline of the forward side hatches, a pick axe, shovel and towing cable and finally the fluted ridges of the engine compartment. At that moment Boden depressed the trigger and the Mark 2 rocked back on its tracks, as the fighting compartment filled with cordite fumes and the Solothurn action of the main armament drove the bolt back on the 2 cm kwk 30.

The solid shot struck the 40 mm sidearmour of the Somua at an angle of fifteen degrees, at a range of twenty metres on the edge of the engine access panel, just above the bolted seam. The round ploughed into the eight cylinder engine igniting three hundred and fifty three litres of petrol contained by the starboard tank as it did so.

Because of the point blank range, the violence of the impact of the solid shot made the self-sealing petrol tank linings ineffective.

However, the fireproof bulkhead separating the engine from the fighting compartment retarded the flames. But enough heat was generated to ignite the propellant of the nearest 47 mm round in the rear ammunition stowage, so that when it exploded its brass cartridge case disintegrated like shrapnel, at the same time projecting the shell upwards to detonate against the steel of the turret cupola. This, in its turn, set off the remaining rounds of HE and Armour Piercing throughout the compartment.

The consequent explosion of these rounds killed the Somua's commander and wireless operator instantly, as they tried to escape through the cast iron portside hatch. It had another consequence, however, since the increasing violence of the explosions split the hull open along the horizontal seam above the track guard, throwing the turret and upper hull up and over like an opening suitcase, the port seam acting as the hinge.

The inferno of blazing fuel was now revealed to Boden who could see that the interior was now nothing more than a blazing white hot furnace.

Had the driver been quicker, he might have escaped; as it was, the sudden loss of engine power coinciding with the direct hit had flung him forward in such a way that his arms and shoulders were tightly jammed through his hatch. The explosions that had followed had not displaced his body, which now hung head downwards through the shattered hull, his neck broken and a tongue of petrol flame incinerating his legs.

Dazed by the heat and the ringing impact of falling steel fragments from the destroyed Somua S35 which now struck and dented the superstructure of the Mark 2 panzer, Boden hoarsely shouted to Wundshammer, pointing down the track away from the blazing tank,

'Get across, damn you, get across!'

Boden was all too well aware of their vulnerable position.

Wundshammer, his head ringing from the repeated crash of explosives, moved forward and away from the burning Somua.

Boden shouted again,

'The track, follow the track! Get on, get away from the bloody thing!'

Wundshammer realised that he could not hear what Boden was saying, and assumed that his voice had been lost in the roar of the engine as he increased throttle.

Seebohn said despairingly,

'Don't you see, you're heading straight into their column!'

'Even if we did, they wouldn't see much, would they?'

By now the burning French tank had ignited the surrounding trees and undergrowth, and this new blaze added to the heavy smoke column produced by the blazing sump oil.

After they had travelled fifty metres down the trail, Boden shouted,

'Turn off, direction south, but only gradually, keep parallel with their track.' To emphasise his meaning he pointed to the right.

Wundshammer nodded dazedly, realising that for some reason he could hear next to nothing.

'Can't you get any more out of the engine?'

'What?'

'Faster!' Boden moved his arm up and down. Now they were well into cover, and Boden ordered a halt at the edge of the wood, when the two man patrol caught up with them.

Buchser said,

'That was an unexpected firework display, and we didn't even bring our anti-tank rifle.'

Boden, too shaken to make any suitable reply, was still recovering from the conflicting stresses of the last five minutes when he had experienced suspense, fear, horror, guilt, triumph and exhilaration simultaneously. Thinking back, he could hardly understand how it was that he was still alive. He was in no mood for jokes, however well intentioned.

'Stick around. You might be invited to de-louse an anti-tank gun position.'

Buchser couldn't be sure whether Boden meant it or not.

'Wherever it is, I prefer it to back there.'

'Oh? And what's happening "back there"?'

'The French 105s have pinpointed our Command post.'

'You mean where we picked you up?'

'That's about it.'

'It sounds time to find out whether the Luftwaffe can do us all a favour. Get through to the Bertas, Seebohn.'

Seebohn switched on his set and began to revolve the Frequency Dial, then he looked up sheepishly at Boden.

'I'm not getting anything.'

'What do you mean, "not getting anything"?'

'We've hit a blind spot, it must be this hill we're on, or the trees. I can't pick up any other station, let alone transmit.'

It was now clear to Boden what had happened to the other panzer patrols outside the wood. Each one had climbed the track, relying on their wireless to call down the Stukas, only to enter a zone of freak conditions from which they were destined never to return. It was no consolation to realise that the French must have similar problems.

Seebohn said,

'Everything would be fine if we were on top of the hill.'

Boden said,

'Of course, and it would make us a wonderful target. Anyway, I don't like hanging about like this, I'm going to the edge of the woods.'

Buchser said,

'A real little fire eater, isn't he? He'll get a monocle and a Division the way he's going, except there's nobody to see.'

Boden made an impatient movement with his hand.

'Come on, Wundshammer, let's get going.'

When Wundshammer came to a halt at the edge of the wood, Boden carefully examined the forward landscape. To begin with it told him little that he did not know already. The bare flat hills swept away to the south, the only difference now being that he could see a checkerboard of maize and vines ahead. The ground between the edge of the wood and the fields beyond had been churned up by panzer tracks. Smoke still hung heavily in the woods around them.

Seebohn said,

'The signal is faint, but it improves the further we advance. At least there is a signal now.'

Then the silence was broken by the thundering roar of tank engines ahead of them.

Boden listened for a moment and said,

'There must be at least thirty.'

Wundshammer swallowed and shook his head.

'What are we doing here?'

Studying the ground again, Boden realised that the French heavies must be hidden in a hollow to the left of the cultivated ground. This feature not only served as a defensive ditch but would also give an open field of fire against any armour seeking the cover of the stream bed.

Conversely, the hollow would be a perfect killing ground for the Stukas. Boden checked the grid reference.

'Are you getting through, Seebohn?'

As he spoke, Boden saw the edge of the fold surge upwards at one point, as six Char Bs heaved themselves menacingly up the reverse slope at 10 kmh, lurching suddenly forward as their half metre tracks dropped to claw into the level ground. Squat and box-like and topped with the French mushroom domed command cupola, they gave an impression of enormous power as they advanced. Examining them through his glasses, Boden could make out the two machine gun positions quite clearly together with the 47 mm SA35 turret armament and the massive muzzle of the forward mounted 75 mm Howitzer.

As they came towards the wood with a slow and ponderous inevitability, they were followed by a second and third line to become a terrifying phalanx.

Already Boden could see the names painted on the glacis plates above the French tricolour; BAYARD, SIMOUN, SIROCCO, MISTRAL, VENDEE and QUERCY. Their cupolas were battened down for battle.

Wundshammer said in a vacuum of deafening silence,

'What happens now? If they keep going the way they are, they won't even have to fire their guns, we'll simply be flattened.'

Seebohn was shouting to the Stuka Controller,

'Target "Yellow", Target "Yellow", twenty French heavies!'

The Controller replied,

'All right, don't lose your shirt. We can hear you. The Bertas are on their way.'

'You needn't sound so relaxed about it; we're being overrun.'

'Don't blame me. You should have linked up with the Forward Artillery Defence Plan and completed your target registration if you had wanted immediate fire support.'

'We've only just got here.'

'Then you'll have to sweat it out. The Bertas are coming.'

As Boden stood in the turret watching the advancing waves of Char Bs he wondered if this was the end. Against such tanks their 2 cm kwk 30 would be about as effective as a waterpistol.

The two infantrymen looked queasy as Buchser said,

'I'm not playing hide and seek with those bastards hanging around. I take it we're not needed any more?'

Boden said,

'I should push off while there's still time.'

'What will you do?'

Boden shrugged.

'What else is there to do but wait.'

'Right, then we're on our way. See you outside the Berlin Metropol after the show.'

Boden gritted his teeth and grimaced as the French heavies continued inexorably on towards the wood. Now they could hardly be more than half a kilometre away, no longer black silhouettes to the naked eye, their drab olive and brown camouflage standing out against the lushness of the surrounding fields.

Buchser however had neglected something which was to prove extremely costly in his case. Although he had adjusted his camouflage to suit his present surroundings, he had not checked his helmet thoroughly enough. The sun, suddenly breaking through the trees, blinked a dull reflection off the green painted steel, sufficient to alert the observing loader in MISTRAL who was watching the wood as they approached. He immediately passed on the possible target to the Renault Commander.

The driver, who came from Bergerac, commented,

'Now we're beating the ground, the rabbits are starting to run.'

The Sous Lieutenant was young and found it difficult to keep up the close relationships the intimacy of the fighting compartment demanded, without loss of face and so he said nothing for a moment. Then finally he gave the order that they had all expected;

'Alert. Target in wood ahead. Infantry. Interdictory Fire. Five rounds 47 mm HE at tree top height. One point five second fuse. Followed by . . . four bursts 100 rounds machine gun fire. In your own time.'

The loader immediately reached forward to pick up his fuse key.

* * *

When Boden heard the first airburst fifty metres to the right he pulled down the turret hatch and said,

'They must have spotted the infantry.'

Wundshammer realised that something was up and said,

'Now we're all for it.'

As MISTRAL's 7.5 Chatellerault and Reibel machine guns sprayed the undergrowth inside the wood at knee height, Buchser, jumping across a fallen log, received two rounds through his right shin bone, so that the shattered fibula stuck lividly awry through the flesh, his foot now nothing more than a useless appendage.

Fortunately or otherwise, Buchser's anterior tibial artery was not severed, so he did not bleed to death, although his jackboot filled with blood. Fighting his constant urge to scream, Buchser began to crawl on all fours back towards the Mark 2 panzer as the silhouettes of the Renaults started to appear at the edge of the wood.

Wundshammer half turned in his seat and said with a blank look to Boden,

'Well, what happens next?' Again he did not hear any answer.

Boden turned to Seebohn.

'Well, Seebohn, what happens next? Where's the bloody Luftwaffe?'

'They've acknowledged.'

Wundshammer said,

'Shall I back up?'

Boden nodded and answered,

'I think you'd better. Make it slow as you can; the wood's under observation.'

Wundshammer found the reverse gear and began to back down towards a clearing which they would have to cross to get access to the bottom of the hill.

'I'll turn in the clearing.'

Seebohn glanced out of his port.

'Don't hang about. We'll make a perfect target.'

Wundshammer said again, expecting a reply,

'I'll turn in the clearing.'

By this time Buchser, exhausted and in great pain, had also reached the clearing. The least movement he made wrenched his broken leg and dangling foot in agony. When he looked for Boden, he could not see the tank, although he could hear the thump of the Maybach engine close by.

Then the pain in his leg became too much and he collapsed face downwards in the pine needles.

As Wundshammer reversed down into the clearing, Boden now re-opened the turret hatch since there were no more airbursts. Once they had turned in the clearing they should be able to escape quickly down the forest tracks using their superior speed.

Wundshammer now nosed back and down into the clearing and began to turn. As Boden looked back he suddenly caught sight of Buchser on the ground below, about to be crushed by the rear port track.

'Hold it!' he shouted to Wundshammer.

The panzer continued to move.

'Stop!' Boden called. 'You're going to hit Buchser.'

Wundshammer turned his head but it was quite clear that he could not hear a word of what Boden was saying.

Boden felt a soft bump under the right hand track and closed his eyes.

Buchser was killed at the same moment as the tracks began to turn, his rib cage crushed under the ten ton dead-weight of the panzer. However he felt nothing except the release from the agony of his shattered leg.

Boden was silent, realising that it was quite pointless to say anything. Wundshammer had clearly been deafened by the sounds from the exploding Somua, maybe he had perforated eardrums. Then he pulled himself together as the panzer's hull began to move to the right.

BAYARD had now reached the edge of the wood, its turret traversing evilly to left and right like the nose of a wolf hound searching for the scent. At length the turret stopped moving and the 47 mm SA 35 armament ranged down towards the grey shadow of the Mark 2 panzer in the clearing.

The air screamed as an armour piercing shot passed through a bank of beech leaves beside the starboard track of the German panzer, scattering them in a momentary wisp of smoke.

Boden shouted to Wundshammer,

'Turn away from the bloody thing! Broadside on, they'll have a perfect target.'

Wundshammer continued on regardless. He had heard nothing.

'For Christ's sake go and do it for him, Seebohn!'

Seebohn bent down into the driver's compartment and tugged at the starboard steering lever and the stern of the Mark 2 began to turn. Then the air outside screamed again and the panzer shook and rattled as though struck by a giant forge hammer as a 75 mm shot smashed through the starboard hull side armour, flashing redly before crossing the wireless operator's station and embedding itself in the armoured duct protecting the air extractor fan.

Seebohn was thrown forward by the impact of the shot, and Boden wrenched his shoulder against the gun support. The Unteroffizier got to his feet and seizing the fire extinguisher doused the still glowing shot.

'Get downhill!' he shouted to Seebohn.

By now Wundshammer began to realise that something was badly wrong, but he still could not quite make out what it was. Seebohn, pointing and waving his arm, was signalling for him to go downhill, which he was going to do anyway.

Above the wood the sky now echoed to a different sound. One by one the shark nosed Bertas dived out of the sun, placing their one thousand kilogram bombs in the phalanx of Char Bs caught in the open at the edge of the wood.

The leader reached the bottom of his almost vertical dive at fifty feet, releasing his bombs, with their 57 second delayed action fuse that would give him enough time to leave the immediate area without being destroyed by the blast of the subsequent explosion.

The 220 kg charge of Amatol TNT created a blast wave that ripped off the forward steel track links of SIMOUN as if they were papiermâché while the casing, bursting at a fifteen degree angle, pierced the 20 mm floor armour of SIROCCO, igniting three HE rounds that were stored at that point, beside the engine. SIROCCO exploded immediately in a plume of smoke, raining red hot fragments down on the surrounding tanks.

At the next pass, tank crews were already leaving the exit ports in the sides of the Char Bs as the Berta leader, having deposited its bomb load, returned to spray them with machine gun fire.

The earth shook again as the delayed action spike bombs detonated at the edge of the wood so that BAYARD, in a vain attempt to take cover, pitched into a bomb crater at an awkward angle; its glacis plate nose down in the earth and the idler wheel main bearing shattered.

Without flak or fighter protection the formation of Char Bs began to disintegrate as individual tank commanders ordered their drivers into or away from the wood, hoping that such deployment would minimise risks to themselves. While obeying an order to make for open ground, the panicking driver of QUERCY crashed headlong into KHAMSIN, toppling it into the hollow from which it had originally emerged. A severed petrol lead continued to pump three hundred and thirty six litres into the engine compartment where it ignited seven seconds later.

Boden saw this rising pillar of fire and smoke against the skyline behind him in a bemused daze. His head was still ringing from the crack of explosions but he could see that BAYARD, their original attacker, had now been knocked out of the battle. In spite of his feeling of relief his mind constantly returned to the image of Buchser's mangled body and the sight of the armour piercing shot glowing inside the tank. Seebohn now sat with his back to it in front of the smashed wireless sets and the litter of loose wires dangling from the bulkhead. He seemed hypnotised by the ten centimetre hole and its implications for him. Had he been sitting in his normal position at the moment of impact, the Char B's shot would have passed through his chest.

Wundshammer, unaware of all that had happened, insulated by the vast caverns of silence in his head, shouted out,

'Look, there's a new pistol port so that Seebohn can kill more Frenchmen!'

Seebohn said sourly,

'Don't make any more jokes, we all missed it by only a hair's breadth.'

Wundshammer could only see the movement of Seebohn's lips and it puzzled him. He shouted back,

'I wonder what happened to our hikers?'

He did not understand the expression that flickered over Boden's face, so he shrugged and drove on thankfully past the notices at the bottom of the wood that warned of the danger from mines.

7 Refugees

When they got back to the ruined cottage which had originally been the command post of 201st Regiment, Boden realised that there had been a change.

To start off with, after the setbacks they had experienced in the confrontations with the Somua and Char Bs, all of them now knew that what had happened up to that point was nothing as to what could happen before the end of the campaign. To some extent it even made Seebohn's presence tolerable.

Wundshammer was also gradually recovering his hearing and reacted to other people's voices, although he did not always understand what they were saying.

At the ruined cottage there was no sign of the Leutnant they had met on their way forward to the ridge. The SS Hauptsturmfuhrer had also disappeared. A number of new shell holes now surrounded the cottage and finally, pulled in on one side of the track that led through the farm, half in and out of the maize, was a driverless Bussing tank transporter.

There was implicit agreement between them after the battle in the fir plantation that they had done enough for the moment. All of them made excuses to themselves not to go on immediately.

Seebohn tidied up the shattered wireless compartment while Boden and Wundshammer inspected the Mark 2's other battle damage.

Their panzer was battle worn on the outside, though otherwise it was quite serviceable. The damage to the engine compartment was not severe in Wundshammer's opinion, the worst consequence being a slight rise in engine temperature due to the partial failure of the extractor fan.

From the outside the Mark 2 looked disreputable and ill used, in spite of the scars being honourable. It was possible to mark their progress from each individual dent, scratch and splinter hole; from the notch left on the turret guard by the sabre of the charging French Captain through to the last and most frightening example of the effectiveness of French armour piercing shot.

Wundshammer, his ears still ringing, then cast his eye over the tank transporter.

'That could do for us. It would save wear and tear on the tracks and driver. But what is it doing here? Is it booby trapped?'

Boden said,

'If we add it to the platoon vehicle strength we'll certainly get to Arras very much quicker. It'll do up to sixty kilometres on the open road.'

'The open road is one thing,' Wundshammer said. 'But what about that?'

They could see now the gleam of windscreens and hear the distant deep throated roar of constant traffic on the road to the south west beyond Thuringy.

Seebohn climbed out by the starboard side port to join them.

'It can't be like that the whole way, and we must re-join the platoon. The Leutnant may need us and it's up to us to get there the quickest way.'

Boden said,

'There's no argument about that. Just which way is the quickest?'

Wundshammer went round to the back of the tank transporter to check the tyre pressures and the brakes as Lansdorff came limping down the road.

'What happened to you?' Boden asked curiously. He still did not know how the two man patrol had got separated.

'Halfway back across the wood the war caught up with me and I was ordered back to bring up the platoon.'

'It looks as though you're out of luck, they seem to have moved on.'

Lansdorff sat down on the stone wall at the roadside and put down his machine pistol before loosening his canteen. He took a pull from it and then, after a pause, asked,

'What's happened to Buchser?'

'Weren't you with him when it happened? I thought you shared the same slit trench.'

'I lost him when the French panzers began to put down that shit in the wood. We'd agreed to RV here if we got separated.'

Boden said carefully,

'We saw him in the wood.'

'What do you mean by that?'

'He got shot up. There was nothing we could do.'

Lansdorff's shoulders suddenly contracted and he shivered.

'What you're really trying to tell me is that you didn't have time to organise a burial detail.'

'That's about the size of it. All hell was being let loose and we were the target. We almost bought it ourselves.' He pointed to the gaping hole in the Mark 2's side armour. 'The French heavies very nearly gunned us down.'

Lansdorff stared at Boden suspiciously, still overwhelmed by shock.

'Is that the whole story?'

Boden shrugged,

'You know what it's like, we've only just come out ourselves and we don't really know whether we're coming or going.'

Lansdorff got up.

'Well, I'm not leaving him to rot in this French shit heap, I'll go and see to him myself. I should have known that the 201st would have gone back to the ridge.'

'We've been ordered to Arras.'

Lansdorff said,

'I hope you enjoy the scenery. Well Herr Unteroffizier, thanks for everything.'

Boden still felt that he hadn't made the position clear.

'He was wounded, we stopped for him, but then he got killed. There was nothing we could do about it.'

'I'm sure he's as grateful as I am, Comrade.'

Boden shrugged and turned away. When he glanced back, Lansdorff was marching up the track towards the wood.

Wundshammer turned to Boden.

'What was all that about? I never knew that Buchser got killed.'

'Forget it, these things happen.'

Wundshammer dropped the subject since it seemed to upset Boden, although he gave him a puzzled look.

'Anyway there doesn't seem to be much wrong with the Bussing.'

The driver plastered mud over the Divisional markings so that a Feldgendarme would really have to be on his toes to spot that all was not as it should be.

Boden said,

'I don't know, shouldn't there be a movement order?'

Wundshammer said,

'Maybe there should under normal conditions. But the hole in the side of the panzer really speaks for itself, and I can always say the extractor fan's blown and we're taking it in to the repair shops. I don't suppose they'll have enough time to argue.'

'Except for the driver who signed for it.'

'He's more than likely dead.'

Wundshammer carefully moved the 10 ton Mark 2 panzer up the transporter's ramps and onto the trailer. Then they secured it with cables to the shackles at the front and back of the hull. The Mark 2 panzer certainly looked as though it was a candidate for the workshops with its buckled track guards and dented turret armour.

Wundshammer said,

'It certainly looks like a write off.'

'Except we'll be heading in the wrong direction, towards the front instead of away from it.'

'I don't know, there's bound to be a repair shop at Arras.'

Then he climbed into the cab of the Bussing Tank Transporter and set the lever in bottom gear.

* * *

The more the recent battle became a memory, the more Seebohn reverted to his earlier, self-righteous and hyper-critical self. What made it worse was that, since now he had really been in action, he counted himself as an expert veteran. But Boden's mind was too occupied with what had happened for him to worry about Seebohn at that particular moment.

They joined the Route Nationale 2 at Vervins before taking the N39 west towards Cambrai. What Wundshammer had pointed out on the main road had been indeed the Wehrmacht Transport columns, but after Vervins it became a different story, as making their way north to La Capelle, they were confronted by an endless column of civilian refugees, all heading south.

Seebohn was quick to point out that the crowds were made up of a mixture of nationalities, Dutch, Belgians and French, all taking the road that would bring them to Paris.

'Where do they think they're going to?' Seebohn asked.

Boden said,

'They're obviously trying to avoid us.'

'You mean the combatant zone?'

'I should have thought that was rather hard to define.'

'From all the French equipment I've seen abandoned, I'd have thought they'd have realised it was all over.'

The ditches were littered with the discarded equipment of French Second Army Infantry formations, packs, rifles, greatcoats and helmets like an unending jumble sale.

'The Winterhelp workers would have a field day,' Wundshammer said.

'Maybe they don't realise that we're German. Perhaps they think the Mark 2's been captured by their own side,' Seebohn said with a rare flash of imagination.

But that thought hadn't crossed Boden's mind either as he sat in the cab staring at the endless procession of cars, carts and plodding people. There were men in blue workmen's overalls, women pushing prams, unarmed French soldiers in their paperboat forage caps and tunics, old people and children, all filled with the blind mass hysteria of escape.

Now Boden noticed that some of the refugees waved to them as they went by, so maybe Seebohn was right or perhaps they thought that the panzer crew was part of a French unit on its way to the Front. How long they would be able to maintain this exercise in self-delusion Boden couldn't tell since the road behind was already crammed with advancing German transport.

As they passed a Belgian bus marked Schaerbeek, Wundshammer said,

'At any rate, the Transporter's faster than that panzer and a much more comfortable ride. My arse is black and blue after the last five days. We should make Cambrai easily today. The others will find the roads just as crowded, but they'll be on tracks, not wheels.'

Boden said,

'It's still a long, long way to the seaside.'

Seebohn seemed to grow tense at the reference to Cambrai.

'Cambrai's near Hamel, isn't it?'

'You're the military history expert. I'll take your word for it.'

'D'you think the English will still be in Cambrai?'

'If they had any sense they'd been sunbathing on Brighton beach, or looking after their Empire, instead of propping up what's left of the French Army.'

Seebohn's eyes began to glow with the fervour they'd come to associate with his political convictions.

'It would be poetic justice, then.'

'What are you on about?' Wundshammer asked angrily. 'What the hell do you mean?'

Wundshammer always found Seebohn particularly offensive when he began to act like a Party official giving a pep talk.

'Then I could avenge my father's memory.'

Wundshammer couldn't restrain his feelings any longer.

'What crap you do talk, Seebohn. Take a good look round you, we're living in 1940, not on some forgotten battlefield twenty five years ago.'

'Sometimes I don't understand your attitude, Wundshammer, there are times when it scarcely seems National Socialist at all.'

'Forget it,' said Wundshammer. 'There's all sorts in the Wehrmacht because everybody has to do their service. I'd sooner it was the Army, personally, rather than the Navy because I never learned to swim, the Rhine's too fast. I don't have any head for heights, so that rules out the Luftwaffe. So I'm in the Army. I like the Army, but I'm only really keen to stay alive. After what happened, back there on the ridge, I'm surprised you don't feel the same. None of us have any business to be alive. We're on borrowed time. You've had a grandstand view of a burning Somua, seen the hikers going to collect their last paypackets and observed what a well directed armour piercing shell can do to our panzer. Isn't that enough?'

Seebohn said,

'Only insofar as it partly redeems the honour of Greater Germany.'

'I only hope we survive all the battles ahead. Really, Seebohn, I don't know how you can talk such balls, you've done about as much fighting as you seem to have done love-making. Both of them add up to a fat round zero. I don't think you've got guts inside, only wind.'

They heard the wail of an approaching siren behind them, and Wundshammer looked in the rear mirror to see a feldgendarmerie motorcyclist, his headlight on beam, blazing up the pave to overtake them on his BMW.

'Does he want to give you a ticket?' Boden asked.

Wundshammer looked anxiously in the mirror once more as he saw a platoon of Mark 3 panzers roaring up behind.

'What shall I do?'

Boden said,

'Pull off the road. They seem to be in a hurry.'

Wundshammer pulled the Transporter off the road and onto the nearside verge at the first opportunity, and the motorcyclist overtook them.

Wundshammer said,

'The civilians don't even seem to want to listen.'

The stream of refugees continued to move apathetically down the road ignoring the oncoming motorcyclist although a few wearily pushed themselves to one side. The biggest blockage was caused by a horse and cart piled high with furniture and mattresses. The old man leading the horse seemed too exhausted to move in, tugging on the rein at the last moment.

As the first of the Mark 3 panzers roared up the road, the old man jerked at the bridle, and the horse turned down into the ditch and the neighbouring field, pulling the loaded cart halfway across the road. Boden now saw that there was a girl lying on the mattress at the back of the cart.

The leading panzer made no attempt to slow down or stop, crashing into the side of the cart, splintering the offside rear wheel and scattering the contents across the road. The girl was thrown to the pave by the impact where she lay in a daze as the second panzer thundered towards her from fifty metres away.

When the crash occurred and the first panzer roared on, the refugee column suddenly froze, standing motionless to gape at the wreckage, and none of them made any attempt to help the girl.

Wundshammer, seeing what had happened, immediately threw open the cab door and, jumping out onto the pave, dragged the girl to the far side verge just a few seconds before the second Mark 2 panzer tore past. The driver then carried her into the shade of a poplar tree, where she lay moaning. This development then attracted a small group of people who stood around her in a half circle, including two French soldiers who had thrown away their rifles and belts. Boden and Seebohn made their way into the circle past an old woman dressed in black, who was pushing a pram that contained a trussed goat.

The driver of the nearest Citroen, who had pulled up and switched off the engine to conserve fuel on the arrival of the German panzers, got out and was already swinging the starting handle.

Wundshammer said,

'She's concussed.'

Seebohn asked,

'How do you know?'

'I know all right; when you work in the motor business you get called out to accidents and that's how you learn about these things.'

One of the French soldiers suddenly called out,

'Assassins!'

His friend whispered to him and then spat. When Seebohn jerked his machine pistol at them they sidled off the road.

'It's always the same with these bastards,' Seebohn complained, 'lend them a helping hand and they'll stab you in the back.'

The rest of the civilians began to shuffle down the road as they saw Seebohn clip in a full magazine.

Boden looked up to see the old man standing beside him staring at the wreckage of the shattered cart. He wore a large white moustache and Boden could see that he was weeping silently. Then Boden asked,

'Does the girl belong to you?'

The old man did not answer so Boden repeated the question and added,

'Someone must look after her.'

But the old man only shrugged wearily before pointing north and saying,

'She is from Belgium. She came because of the bombers.'

'Where are you going?'

'Paris.'

'There is still fighting on the Aisne.'

The old man shrugged again.

'What difference does that make? There is fighting everywhere and now we've lost everything. I will go to my wife's cousin at Limoges.'

'But what about the girl?'

'She needs attention, anyone can see that. There is a Refugee Rest Centre at Chapelle, along the road you're going.'

Boden said,

'Then we better take her to Chapelle.'

Seebohn said,

'I don't see it's any of our business. It would be much simpler if we left her here.'

Wundshammer looked up.

'What's the matter, Seebohn? Do girls bother you or something? If we leave her out here anything could happen.'

Seebohn said,

'Well just don't involve us in a riot, these people may think you're going to take her off and rape her.'

'That's not my style, although I expect you were too busy fiddling about with your wireless set half the night to notice.'

Seebohn frowned and then crossed the road to the Bussing cab.

'Where are you going to put her?'

'On the bunk at the back of the cab.'

Wundshammer put the girl under the blanket at the back. She had dark hair and a small, attractive face. She wore a skirt and jersey, as though she had been camping. Boden thought she looked quick-witted, but if that was really the case how had she become involved in this panic exodus to nowhere?

After they'd all got in, Wundshammer said,

'She's cold.'

Boden said,

'She's probably in shock. You better keep her warm.'

Boden was surprised by Wundshammer's concern, but put it down to the fact that he might have saved her life. As he started the engine he turned to Boden and asked,

'What unit were those panzers from?'

'Totenkopf SS. They seem to have acquired some armour.'

Seebohn said,

'That's because they're top of the Führer's class, and rightly so.'

After two kilometres of bumping along the uneven road, the girl stirred and asked weakly,

'Where are you taking me?'

Her French had an accent that Boden couldn't quite place.

'You are my prisoner,' Seebohn said by way of a joke but his sense of humour seemed lost on the girl.

'What is to happen to me? Am I to be shot?'

Seebohn, who knew just about enough French to be able to conduct this kind of conversation, laughed and said,

'Oh, no, nothing like that; we are taking you to a clinic.'

'I feel all right,' the girl's voice had an underlying note of hysteria.

Wundshammer said,

'The cart you were in was hit by a tank. You had quite a bad fall.'

'Oh yes, the cart.'

Boden asked,

'Where are you from?'

'From Rotterdam. We were bombed out.'

Seebohn said,

'The fortunes of war.'

'The misfortunes of war, more like.'

Boden asked,

'Where are you trying to get away to?'

'Anywhere where there is no war. Spain, North Africa.'

Seebohn said,

'You should not worry about such things. The war is almost finished. The Führer has announced that there will be a Peace Rally at the Party Conference next September. France is now finished, and soon England will throw in its hand. Now that the whole rotten swindle is exposed, we Germans can start to drag Europe into the twentieth century. Rebuild it.'

The girl said rather unexpectedly,

'That's the sort of talk I like to hear. A new start.'

Seebohn smiled, flattered by her agreement.

'When the war is won, a new start; a new order. Here, will you take some wine?'

Wundshammer and Boden exchanged surprised glances as he handed the girl his canteen. Boden began to wonder whether she had been as badly hurt as they had all thought.

'Thanks,' said the girl. 'I will.'

'New friends, new comrades,' Seebohn went on in his irritating, sentimental vein, winking meaningfully at Boden and Wundshammer.

He took the canteen when the girl handed it back and had a drink himself, although he didn't offer it to the others.

'No objections, I hope, Herr Unteroffizier?'

'None in the least,' said Boden.

'Good.'

Out of the corner of his eye, Boden saw that the girl was stroking the back of Seebohn's neck.

She said silkily,

'You Germans are such good fighters. No wonder the British and French haven't a chance.'

'That's because we'll accept risks as part of the honour of being a soldier.' He paused. 'Have you seen the British?'

'Oh yes, they were always retreating.'

'I have a score to settle with the British.'

The girl noticed his frown and changed the subject.

'What is your name?'

'Mine is Fritz. The driver is called Willy and the Unteroffizier next to him, Micki.'

'My name is Annette.'

'I like that name, it is elegant.'

'I too have always loved Germany, the Rhine and the historic cities.'

'It's true we have the purest culture in Europe.'

Wundshammer sighed as Boden said,

'Oh do shut up, Seebohn, and keep it for your "Strength through Joy" meetings.'

Seebohn was silent for a moment as Annette asked,

'Please, can you ask the driver to stop at the next haystack?'

'Whatever for?'

'That's not the sort of question a gentleman ever asks a lady.'

'Forgive me, then, for asking.'

'Don't worry, there's no need to be so correct. I must go for a walk, you know, make pee-pee.' Annette giggled provocatively. 'Since I'm a prisoner I'll need an escort. At a distance, of course, to see that I don't escape.'

Seebohn smiled knowingly and glanced over to Boden and Wundshammer with an air of triumph.

When they came to the next wood, Wundshammer drew the Tank Transporter in to the roadside in silence and Seebohn pointedly took up his machine pistol with a businesslike flourish.

'Don't worry, if it frightens you, I can always unload it.'

Annette giggled again and said,

'You mustn't say things like that.'

Climbing down off the front mudguard to the step below the cab, Annette ran into difficulties with her skirt, and so revealed a long section of stockinged leg to Seebohn.

When they had gone Boden shrugged once and then lit up an Eckstein. Then they sat together in silence, watching the constant stream of refugees walking past them on the other side of the road.

After five minutes had gone by Wundshammer said,

'D'you know something? I don't know about that Annette. D'you think everything's all right and she's all she says she is?'

'That doesn't amount to much. She was your idea but she certainly seems to have taken to Seebohn.'

'Considering she seemed to be concussed, she's made a miraculous recovery. I rather doubt whether she needs a doctor at all.'

'Seebohn's perfectly capable of looking after himself.'

'Yes, but she certainly laid it on a bit thick. What on earth could she see in him?'

Wundshammer reached round and felt under her blanket for a moment before pulling out a strap handbag.

'This needs some investigation. I thought she'd left something behind.'

'Her handbag,' said Boden. 'It's normal.'

Wundshammer put the bag on his knee and opened it. Inside it contained a mirror, lipstick, powder compact and comb. There was also a dark brown carnet of railway tickets valid for the journey from Amsterdam to London via Calais, and tucked away in a pocket at the back was a British passport.

'Come on,' Boden said resignedly. 'We'd better go and rescue Seebohn, or we'll never hear the end of it.'

They found Seebohn inside the wood leaning against a tree, minus his trousers, underpants and machine pistol.

Wundshammer said,

'I suppose the honour of Greater Germany stopped you

from calling us up as reinforcements?'

Seebohn glared at Wundshammer.

'She was an English spy.'

Boden smiled.

'She was certainly English, but where did she go?'

He looked quizzically at the contrast between Seebohn's naked, lily white legs and his immaculate black tunic, and found it so incongruous that he began to laugh.

Seebohn frowned and said vaguely,

'She made off south across the fields.'

Wundshammer said,

'If she's a spy we'll have to stop and make a detailed report to Field Security the first chance we have. It'll be our duty to tell them exactly how we found you.'

Seebohn said sharply,

'In that case, there's nothing to report.'

Boden said,

'I can see what you mean, now you mention it. But where are your trousers? The Herr Leutnant won't want to have you like that on parade.'

'She wanted me to take them off. Then when the action was starting to get interesting, she stuck the machine pistol in my gut. She seemed to know how to use it all right.'

Wundshammer said,

'Too bad. She was quite a looker. I wouldn't have minded a tumble in the hay with her myself.'

Seebohn pondered for a moment and then suggested,

'Maybe we should try searching for her.'

'No,' said Boden. 'We've wasted enough time.'

However, Seebohn was determined to find someone other than himself to blame for what had happened.

'If that fat, stupid Rhinelander hadn't picked her up to start off with, I'd never have landed in this mess.'

'Is that right?' Wundshammer replied.

'Hell,' said Seebohn. 'How was I to know?'

Boden said as they walked back to the Tank Transporter,

'Well, there's something else for you to chalk up against the British.'

'You're absolutely right. One is a fool to trust them.'

'Still,' said Boden. 'She could have shot you, and she didn't do that.'

When they got to Chapelle, Seebohn smashed the window of the General Store and took a pair of dark blue trousers, the only available colour, since his kit was in store at Regiment. They were the only pair that he could find, and he took them–although they were much too small and made of denim–because they were better than nothing at all.

'That's what comes of being nice to people,' Seebohn said. 'The next Englishman I see won't just get a bullet, he'll get the whole magazine.'

Boden decided to say nothing, although he could tell that Seebohn really meant it.

8 Arras

On the Route Nationale 39 they came across their Unit sign for the first time.

'Not far from the Platoon,' said Wundshammer.

'Not so far from the sea either,' said Seebohn. 'I heard on the six o'clock news on the forces programme that we've all but arrived at the Channel.'

31st Regiment's vehicle park was in the 7th Panzer Division area close to the village of Croisilles on the Bapaume Road. The area containing the panzers, workshops and the administrative tail which was still arriving was overlooked by the Hospice of a Marist Convent. As Wundshammer rolled in with the Tank Transporter there were sarcastic catcalls and derisive whistles from the other panzer crews.

Hans Redwitz, who drove 4 panzer and who was walking to the mobile aid post, shouted,

'What's kept you? Been for a spin down the Autobahn?'

Boden ignored the comments, keeping his eyes open for the other two tanks of 6 Platoon. Richter, Munchausen and Stossen were crouched over the engine of Number 5 panzer, but the only sign of 4 panzer was Redwitz. Then he saw the other Mark 2 being refuelled by Haagen and Loeker.

'Why isn't Redwitz with you?'

'He's on his way to First Aid. Unfortunately, it's nothing serious. The silly bastard was fooling about with a French pineapple grenade when the detonator went off. Luckily for him it didn't ignite the main charge, but it did singe his eyebrows.'

'Where's the Leutnant?'

'Directing everyone to panic stations. We're moving up to the front in ten minutes, to stop the gap.'

'Has there been a breakthrough?' Boden asked incredulously.

'Believe it or not, it's the British. Not at all cricket. They've got up enough nerve to attack south of Arras, and our anti-tank guns haven't been able to stop their armour.'

'And they expect us to do any better?'

'I suppose they think we won't make such easy targets.'

Boden felt his stomach tighten again.

'We've just had our first introduction to taking on the heavies.'

Haagen looked up with interest.

'I hadn't heard that.'

'We were sent on a recce near Laon when we came face to face with the French. I can tell you, it wasn't amusing.'

'All we've seen of the French to date is abandoned equipment.'

Boden asked,

'Have you seen these British wonder panzers?'

'Only through field glasses. You'd better go and chat with the Leutnant.'

Boden found Von Dressen pacing nervously up and down.

'Oh, it's you, Boden. So you made it after all. You've been out of contact.'

'We came as fast as we could, Herr Leutnant. Our wireless packed up when the French scored a bullseye.'

'Well, I see you arrived in style, so at least your panzer should be in working order. The pave's knocked hell out of the tracks of all the others. Anyway everyone's got to get out on the road. You won't have much time, you'll have to visit the petrol point, draw some more ammunition and iron rations.'

Boden said,

'It's certainly all happening.'

'Quite right, there's not much time to stop the rot south of Arras.'

'How are casualties?'

'Nothing serious in the Platoon. The infantry took a beating because there was no armour in support and nobody dreamed that the anti-tank gunners would develop a problem.'

'We need a new wireless set and air extractor unit.'

'You might get fixed up in time before we move off, but I doubt it. You'd better talk to maintenance.'

Boden was subdued when he went back to the Tank Transporter, for judging by the way that Von Dressen was talking, the battle outside Arras certainly sounded touch and go. The Unteroffizier had been right to think that it all seemed a little too easy from the time they crossed the French frontier. The French were one thing, and not all their equipment was obsolete, as they had discovered to their cost, but the success of the British armour sounded frightening. He was no more reassured when he talked to Nacwicz, who was in charge of the Maintenance Unit.

'It's a different proposition. The British are organised, their tanks are worthwhile, and they want to fight; what's more they're backed up by infantry. They're fighting for survival now we've cut their supply lines north. All they've got left is their petrol depot at Abbeville and the BEF Field Supply at Doullens. Once those have gone, they've had it, their army will grind to a halt. They're not capable of air-lifting in their necessary supplies, and the Channel ports have been blasted so they can't be supplied by sea. Their main supply bases were Le Havre and Cherbourg, but with the French in a shambles they've no chance of relying on them. So really this is the last chance they have of making it work. Once we reach the sea, they'll know it's only a matter of time and all they can do is retreat.'

Boden said,

'They seem to have done quite well so far.'

'That's because, in spite of useless officers, the British are like us; they don't give up easily once they've put their minds to it.'

'I don't see what they're fighting for.'

'Neither does anyone else But they don't want to change, and they're used to giving orders from the safety of their island. They're run by capitalists who have no real respect for the working man as we have in Germany, and their class structure is as rigid as the Hindus.'

Boden said,

'This is all very well but what about my panzer?'

'The extractor fan won't matter, except you may get a slight rise in engine temperature. It's nothing to worry about. But there are no spare sets, although some may come in tonight. Don't worry about that, you'll be able to go out and run rings round them. Come and see me again once you're back.'

When he left the maintenance unit, Boden found that Von Dressen was nervously haranguing the Platoon.

'This may not be so easy.'

Richter said,

'Well, so far we haven't done too badly; nine days from the Rhine to Arras. I call that some kind of record. They spent four years trying to do that before, and even then they didn't make it.'

'I agree. Anyway, we're going in to support 18th Rifle Regiment. In case you hadn't heard, the SS has been badly knocked about out there, so things can't have been that easy.'

Loeker had been involved in arguments with the SS in beer halls near the training barracks, and did not like them.

'They're amateurs, all chat and no action. All they're good for is singing the Horst Wessel song.'

Von Dressen said,

'This isn't a political meeting, so you can forget all that. We're going to move up the Bapaume Road towards Arras. It's ideal tank country, flat and open. If we stay overnight there could be a mist first thing in the morning, which could inhibit the activities of the Bertas.'

Panzer 6 led the way to begin with, followed by 4 and 5 panzers. To the north west a cloud of smoke marked the burning centre of Arras. In the distance, Boden could see the smudge of the Doullens Railway, and through his glasses he sighted a bombed out train, its buckled locomotive halfway down the slope of the embankment.

After a time Boden's panzer was overtaken by the others. Wundshammer did not want to take any chances with the damaged air extractor unit and kept his speed down, although the engine temperature had only risen four or five degrees. Von Dressen followed on in his command panzer.

As they advanced along the road beside a cabbage field, Boden was aware of the procession of ambulances heading towards them from the fighting zone. Immediately behind the platoon was a Regiment of 1.55 mm guns towed by tractors, but these turned off at Wancourt.

Wundshammer shouted above the roar of the Maybach engine,

'Any signs of the eighty eights?'

Boden said,

'We seem to be on our own now.'

'Where are we going?'

'We're supposed to be advancing south of Wancourt towards St Martin.'

They passed a cemetery on their right, hedged off with privet and containing row upon row of German crosses. The sign over the gate simply said, 'Arlcourt'.

'What's that?' Wundshammer asked.

'You'd better ask Seebohn. It looks like a monument to our efforts round here in 1916. He'll tell you all about it, but kindly don't reserve a place in it for me.'

Seebohn looked solemnly out. He felt redundant without his wireless set, since there was nothing useful for him to do. Being unoccupied made him even more nervous in the face of the possibility of the oncoming battle.

When he saw the cemetery, he saluted theatrically.

Boden remarked,

'Let's hope we won't join our fallen comrades.'

Seebohn announced confidently,

'There'll be no more war after this, and we'll be back to the fatherland in another three months, you'll see. This is a historic moment.'

As he spoke, the ground ahead erupted in a pillar of flame.

'D'you think we've been spotted?'

'What's your guess?'

Von Dressen was now signalling them to fan out from the turret of his command panzer. Needing no further invitation, Boden shouted to Wundshammer,

'Get into the fields!'

'Anything you say.'

The Mark 2 panzer bucked across the roadside ditch, tearing up the barbed wire and corkscrew picquets making up the fence that were another legacy of the 14–18 war.

Number 5 panzer, commanded by Richter, was now a hundred metres away to their left, making for a belt of rusty barbed wire.

'Where's Richter going?' Wundshammer asked.

Richter started to move parallel to the obstacle in the direction of a terrace of derelict houses, obviously relics of an earlier battle that nobody had bothered to clear away. Boden now left the fields and came to rough, uncultivated ground covered with coarse grass, passing a sign that read, NO ENTRY – DANGER OF DEATH.

Wundshammer said uneasily,

'That's a laugh – I've read that somewhere before.'

Boden said,

'They must have fenced off part of the old battlefield to make a tourist attraction.'

Wundshammer changed down and ploughed slowly over the uneven ground. Ahead, Boden saw a grass covered crater filled with half buried and rusting cylinders.

'For God's sake, keep away from that!'

Wundshammer called out,

'I can't hear you. Do you want me to stop? I thought we were supposed to advance to contact.'

'No, just be careful what you drive over. There could be something lethal buried in this litter.'

'Why can't we find a better place?'

'That's what I'm trying to do.'

Then they crossed a half filled trench and the ground seemed to level off. Boden was just beginning to feel relieved when there was a dampened thud and the ground shook beneath them. Boden looked across to where Number 5 panzer had ground to a halt halfway across a crater. Boden saw Richter get out to inspect the damage.

Boden said grimly,

'We better go and see if Richter needs us.'

Wundshammer obediently turned towards Richter's panzer. When they came up, Richter said angrily,

'Almost nine hundred kilometres non-stop, and that idiot Munchausen has to drive over a museum piece mine that's still active!'

Boden could see Munchausen's face white through the driver's port. Blood was running from his mouth.

'Looks like he's been hurt.'

Munchausen said between clenched teeth,

'It's my ankle, I can't move it. I think it must be broken.'

The blast of the exploding mine, although not penetrating the 4 mm floor armour, had thrown Munchausen forward awkwardly, fracturing his left foot; at the same time his face was slammed against the inside of the glacis plate.

'You better call up First Aid.'

Munchausen said nervously,

'Just get me out of here, please; I can't move.'

Richter lit an Eckstein and pushed it through the visor into Munchausen's mouth.

'If you insist.'

'I insist all right. If we're suddenly caught with our trousers down, you'll have to dig my grave. I just won't be able to make it out of here by myself.'

'O.K. Unlock your overhead hatch. Do you want a morphine shot?'

'I just want out of this cast iron death trap!'

The radio crackled and Von Dressen said over the 5 panzer wireless,

'Why have you dropped out, Richter?'

'We've hit a mine and Munchausen's broken his ankle.'

'What's Boden doing with you?'

'We'll have to mend the track and I can't manage it quickly with less than five.'

'Right, as soon as you've fixed it, make for the Tilloy crossroads.'

'Yes, Herr Leutnant.'

By this time the hatch above the driver's head was open, and Munchausen painfully wriggled his head and shoulders through it. Boden and Richter climbed on the hull and each gripped one of Munchausen's shoulders.

'Are you ready?'

Munchausen nodded numbly. Then the two panzer men heaved, pulling him up out of the hatch so that a moment later he was sitting on the hull. In spite of himself Munchausen gave out an agonising scream.

'One more time.'

They pulled simultaneously, so that now he stood on the upper glacis on his good leg, trembling and shivering. Boden cut away the bottom of his trouser leg to reveal a blue white ripple of displaced bone just under the skin surface.

Boden said,

'I don't know what you've got to complain about, they'll probably send you to convalesce in Baden-Baden.'

Through his teeth Munchausen shouted,

'Fuck Baden-Baden! What the hell's the good of Baden-Baden? I want to see the sights in Paris. That's what I've been sweating my guts out for.'

Boden said,

'Well they wouldn't be much good to you anyway, with a broken leg like that.'

They lowered Munchausen off the panzer, and Boden slid down the side to inspect the damage to 5 panzer's track.

Ahead of them the late afternoon sky was cloudless. Suddenly Boden was aware of two infantry, thirty metres to their front, retreating against the distant crackle of machine gun fire. Boden guessed that it was a British machine gun, since the rhythm was methodical and slow. While Richter was removing spare track links from the front of his panzer, Boden shouted to the infantry to come over.

'What's going on?'

'What does it look like, Comrade, we're falling back.'

Boden raised his eyebrows when he saw that one of them wore SS collar patches.

'I always understood that you were the spearhead against the enemies of Greater Germany.'

'Why don't you fuck off, Corporal? That's just pigshit! If you were back there you'd find out why soon enough.'

'It won't be long before we are.' Beyond the two SS men Boden could make out other scattered groups of infantry falling back, one group dragging an anti-tank gun.

'You'd better run along now,' Boden said, 'and join your friends.'

One of the SS men spat angrily, while the other called over his shoulder as they made off,

'I wish you joy with the British panzers! Armour piercing bounces off their armour at a hundred metres, just like a tennis ball.'

Boden said,

'How I hate the arrogant bastards! They'll probably get a Führer citation for making a fighting withdrawal.'

Then he called to Seebohn,

'Watch your front and tell me when you see something. There's going to be some action.'

Even at that distance he could observe the nervous rise and fall of Seebohn's adam's apple.

'All right, Richter, let's get the track fixed.'

To do this Richter climbed into the driver's seat and edged the panzer gently back until the broken links were exposed. Four would have to be changed since, apart from the fracture, two had been distorted by the blast.

Boden took the sledgehammer and started to knock out the linkpins, while Stossen manhandled the rest of the track off the return wheels, helped by Wundshammer, so that it stretched out like a long snake behind the panzer.

Two orderlies, wearing Red Cross brassards, ran over to Munchausen. One of them shouted to Boden,

'We'll have to get him out of here fast!'

'It's becoming quite a habit today.'

'If you look over there to the right, you'll see why.'

Boden stood up and looked towards the north. Beyond the belt of rusting wire he could make out the silhouette of an unfamiliar panzer.

'They're wandering about all over the place, no-one seems to know how to stop them, the anti-tank guns have no effect.'

'Nor do the SS. You better remove the casualty.'

'We're on our way.'

The British Mark I Infantry Tank moved forward uncertainly and hesitated, as though the Commander wasn't quite sure what he was expected to do. Then it turned side on, rocking on its suspension like a grasshopper; it was painted a dark green and Boden could make out the short barrel of a machine gun projecting from its circular turret, with a grenade launcher on either side. The name DERVISH was painted in white letters on the front of the driver's compartment. After a moment it continued north, as though searching for a way round the belts of barbed wire. Boden shouted to Richter,

'We'll have to look sharp.'

By this time Stossen had removed the linkpins and, taking out the damaged track plates, had put new ones in position. All that was needed now was for the track to be folded back over the idler wheel and the pins hammered home. Boden hoped that both panzers blended with the battleground junk with which they were surrounded.

Boden, keeping his eye on the British tank, said,

'Let's wrap it up, shall we?'

'I'm with you there,' Richter answered.

A final blow from the sledgehammer secured the track.

'Now at least we're mobile.'

The British Infantry Tank paused at a break in the wire, as though the commander was trying to evaluate the track marks.

Richter said,

'Christ! Here comes another of the bastards.'

Boden looked to where he was pointing and saw a second tank, this time followed by British infantry, advancing at walking pace across a field of kale five hundred metres to the south west.

'Maybe it's lucky for us that we fetched up here; we can play hide and seek in this mess till nightfall.'

'You really think so?'

'Why not? In any case, it's two against two.'

Seebohn shouted,

'Shall I open fire?'

Boden looked through his glasses towards this latest arrival as the British Cruiser headed for the wire. There were two ancillary machine gun turrets built into the hull forward of the main turret, and the suspension seemed more modern than that of the Infantry tank. However, the Unteroffizier noted that the armour was riveted rather than welded. Its angular turret carried a two pounder gun and another machine gun and the name GREYHOUND was painted across the olive and dark green camouflage. It was the larger of the two tanks, and flew a green flag from its wireless antenna.

Boden said to Richter,

'You better let them know we're here in a minute. I'll get inside these houses.'

Richter said,

'I'll reverse hull down to the crater.'

'O.K.'

'Regiment knows what's going on. They've signalled that they're forming an anti-tank screen on an axis behind the Hendecourt–Lecluse road.'

Boden said,

'Let's hope it's sooner rather than later. Did they mention eighty eights?'

'They didn't go into detail.'

Boden ordered Wundshammer to back up to the remains of the terraced houses that stood incongruously at the centre of the former trench system. Boden guessed that at one time they had been built for factory workers, but had been abandoned from the time of the armistice. The terrace was built in a depressing yellow brick, broken by a pattern of red diagonals; sections of the blue-black roof slates were missing.

'Quick, round the back and in through the kitchen.'

'But the wall will collapse.'

'That's the whole idea. We'll all feel safer with six feet of rubble between us and whatever they are out there.'

By now the British tank, nervous about crossing the rusting belt of barbed wire, had slowed down.

Boden's panzer crashed in through the yellow brickwork at the back of the end house after crossing an overgrown back garden, tall with cow parsley and other weeds. The section of wall as far as the joists above collapsed in a cloud of plaster dust at the impact, before Wundshammer edged in bottom gear across the floor tiles of the downstairs living room.

'Take it easy.'

Wundshammer brought the panzer to a halt as the glacis plate touched the front wall.

Boden clambered out of the turret and, taking the sledge hammer, stood on the hull and started to loosen the brickwork at the level of the mantlet to the left of the front door and window.

'Where's Richter?' Seebohn asked.

'Squatting in a shell hole not far from here. What's it feel like to be re-fighting the trench war?'

'I don't think that's very funny.'

'It's not meant to be; it's a statement of fact.'

By this time Boden had displaced a five foot section of brickwork, forming a narrow slit through which it was now possible to sight and lay the 2 cm kwk 30.

The British Infantry Tank cautiously began to cross the belt of wire, having nosed its way in through a gap.

Boden could see that Richter was now in position, his Mark 2 Panzer hull canted across the overgrown shell hole, his 2 cm gun trained towards the British Mark I Infantry tank on the right, the barrel at maximum depression so that it was now almost parallel to the ground.

Seebohn asked,

'What are the targets, and when should I attack?'

Boden said,

'Use the MG 34, and the principal target will be the British Cruiser – spray the visors, it might make them change direction and go and try somewhere else. If they haven't vision blocks, you could even score a bull's eye through an unguarded slit.'

'What about the other targets?'

'All right, Seebohn, you can attack their infantry, but for God's sake make sure you don't miss.'

While Seebohn had been adjusting the sight and checking the feedbelt, Boden clambered through the debris and over to Number 5 panzer.

'While Seebohn concentrates on the infantry, make the British Infantry tank your target. There aren't any more targets this side.'

'I certainly can't bear on the Cruiser from my present position.'

'Yes, we're taking care of that. I just don't want to give the game away too soon. Your target looks as though it's only armed with a machine gun.'

By now the British infantry were walking forward to the furthest belt of wire, spreading out to get round the sides. Boden judged that they could not be more than two hundred and fifty metres away.

'Put in your first shot after we've fired. If you start the ball rolling, their infantry will go to ground.'

Richter said,

'We could do with a few of those SS, right now.'

'There are lots of things we could do with, including eighty eight millimetre guns, they crack any armour. But at least we're not short of ammo.'

Boden turned to the terrace of houses to signal Seebohn to start shooting, by raising and lowering his pistol above his head in the conventional infantry attack signal.

The Unteroffizier heard Seebohn's MG34 with its sound of tearing calico as he reached the corner of the houses.

Then, ten seconds later Boden heard the whistle of a grenade, delivered from the British Infantry Tank's launcher, before he was blasted to the ground by the one kilo charge of TNT that exploded with a roar somewhere to his right. Picking himself up, he found not only that his knee was twisted and his side bruised, but also that a scalpel-sharp shrapnel splinter had impacted in the muscle inside his right elbow, jarring the bone so that his whole arm was in agony, blood soaking his uniform sleeve.

However, Seebohn had taken careful aim, and the left wing of the advancing British infantry was decimated before they realised what was happening. Seebohn swept their extended order line once more as they dropped to cover.

Shortly afterwards, in a daze, Boden twice heard the crack of Richter's 2 cm kwk 30, but when he staggered back to the house he found to his astonishment that the British Infantry Tank was still advancing. Using his left hand, the Unteroffizier trained his glasses on the British tank, trying to work out what had gone wrong. It was unbelievable that it was possible to miss, firing from a static position at a range of under two hundred metres. The British Infantry Tank continued to grind on, ploughing through the swathes of rusting barbed wire.

Then Richter fired again and this time Boden saw that his shot struck home. The British Infantry Tank shuddered as Boden observed a cup-like scar gouged out of the nose of its frontal armour. At a hundred and fifty metres the 2 cm shot should penetrate 40 cm of armour and the crew should now be destroyed inside their blazing tank.

As the British tank continued its advance, Boden waited for it to return fire, but all he could see was the traverse, to right and left of the Vickers 303 machine gun, as it sprayed the area beside Richter's panzer.

Boden turned to Wundshammer, his forearm dripping with blood.

'The British have an impregnable moving machine gun. It looks as though we can't stop it, but it can do no damage to us.'

'That's what those SS must have meant about them overrunning the anti-tank guns.'

Then Wundshammer caught sight of Boden's arm.

'Get the First Aid and fix me a tourniquet, I'm losing blood.'

Wundshammer pursed his lips as he saw the jagged piece of shrapnel embedded in Boden's elbow joint. 'I'll do what I can.'

'That's all I ask.'

Wundshammer immediately staunched the flow of blood by applying the tourniquet at the brachial artery.

'Not too tight, I don't want to lose my arm. God knows how long we'll be out here.'

'I quite understand.'

Now there was a loud crash to the left of the Mark 2 panzer, and a section of wall crumbled and fell away. Boden looked cautiously through the window which had shattered at the impact of the hard shot to find that the second British Cruiser Tank was no further than one hundred and twenty metres away.

The British hard shot, having brought down a section of wall, embedded itself in a ceiling joist, glowing red hot, so that soon flames began to flicker along the laths which had now been exposed.

Wundshammer said,

'I marked the flash from the triple turreted panzer. They must think that we're only an MG nest.'

Boden could see that this would be logical enough. Seebohn's sudden attack on the British Infantry must have been carefully noted by the Cruiser commander. Seebohn didn't seem quite certain as to what to do next having evoked this response.

Boden said,

'You wanted to stir up the hornet's nest, Seebohn, and because I can't move my right arm effectively I'll have to ask you to destroy it.'

'Shall I have a crack at them with the 2 cm?'

'No, keep that in reserve. Keep on spraying the visor slits, and then perhaps they'll do something stupid. The closer they come, the better the chances are of knocking the thing out.'

Seebohn said tightly,

'Anything you say.'

Now Boden could see the heads of the British infantry as they bobbed up and down, picking their way along the lanes the British tanks had forced through the wire.

Boden saw sparks shower off the front hull of the British Infantry Tank as Richter once more attempted the impossible at under a hundred metres.

Wundshammer began to mutter nervously,

'Why doesn't he aim for the track?'

The Unteroffizier, trying to suppress the pain in his arm, found himself comparing the panzer duel with the net men and heavily armoured fighters in the Roman gladiatorial shows.

The battle seemed evenly balanced because of the limitations on either side. The British Infantry Tank was slow, had heavy armour and one machine gun. The German panzers were fast, carried comparatively light armour and were armed with a 2 cm gun. Then Boden suddenly realised that, despite its superior armament, the British Cruiser Tank had, by this time, overtaken the British Infantry Tank. Although the increase in speed was not spectacular, it could only mean to Boden that the Cruiser Tank carried lighter armour, particularly because of the three machine guns and the two pounder it was carrying.

Seebohn again desperately began to spray the front of the British Cruiser with the MG 34, although it was difficult to maintain a consistent aim on such a moving target.

Boden said,

'Concentrate on the centre of the hull and keep the driver occupied.'

The British tanks were closing in, and Boden could sense Seebohn's desperation. The Unteroffizier gloomily suspected that Seebohn was re-enacting the events of 1918, and even playing out his father's experiences. Seebohn had now stepped up the rate of machine gun fire, even though he knew that this would soon overheat the barrel, which would then have to be changed.

There was another crack above their heads, and this time part of the ceiling fell in behind them, bringing with it a cloud of dust that mingled with the smoke from the burning timber behind.

Boden said quickly,

'Have you loaded?'

'Yes.'

'Then try an armour piercing round.'

Boden waited for the dustcloud to subside as Seebohn fidgeted with the sight.

'What's holding you up?'

'It's hopeless! I can't see properly.'

'We'll all be enjoying eternal darkness if you carry on at this rate!'

Outside, a finger of afternoon sunshine backlit the British

Cruiser's silhouette as it kept on blazing away with its three machine guns.

Then Boden said,

'Haven't you thought what will happen, once the Tommies are loose in this position? They won't be exactly pleased to see us, and they'll be carrying bloody great blocks of TNT to blow us up with, as though their grenades weren't bad enough.'

'I know, we haven't a chance.' Seebohn's teeth were chattering.

Boden said suddenly,

'Here, get out of the way for God's sake and let me do it.'

Seebohn muttered something inaudible and crouched down in the corner beside the engine compartment.

'We're cutting it pretty fine.'

Another round from the closing British Cruiser brought down the wall beside the window and exposed the port side of the Mark 2 panzer's hull. Boden noticed that the impregnable Infantry Tank had now stopped and was methodically spraying the area beside Richter's panzer and launching grenades.

Boden checked the sight and felt for the firing button with his left hand. When he depressed it there was only an empty click.

'I thought you said you'd loaded up?'

'Yes, I put a new belt on the MG while you were with Richter.'

Without comment, Boden leaned back, his right arm on fire and slipped in the magazine. Controlling his nausea he checked the sight, aiming at the junction of the Cruiser's turret and the hull armour that now filled the Zeiss aperture.

'Let's hope it works this time.'

'What do you mean by that?' Wundshammer asked anxiously.

Boden said,

'The British seem to go in for heavy armour. That's why I've been holding back the 2 cm right up to the last minute, though I must say I hadn't exactly counted on waiting until

I could see the whites of their eyes.'

When he looked through the forward visor he could clearly make out the name GREYHOUND painted on the turret.

A jet of flame hung momentarily at the muzzle of the British Cruiser's two pounder and Boden and Wundshammer felt a tremendous slap as the hard shot, ricocheting onto the Mark 2 panzer's track guard, was deflected on a course parallel to the side of the hull, so that it slipped along the side of the fighting compartment, smashing through the toolboxes and spare track links.

Boden's ears were ringing as he depressed the firing mechanism in reply, using his left hand.

The 2 cm hard shot penetrated the 14 mm frontal armour of the British Cruiser at a velocity of over eight hundred metres a second. The slight metal barrier it struck simply caused the soft steel nose of the round to splatter as the tungsten core smashed into the turret, decapitating both the tank commander and the main turret gunner and removing four ribs and the left collar bone from the loader's thorax as he was slipping the next round into the breech.

In spite of the spread of the shot, the round continued through the 14 mm turret back armour, whining and humming like a distorted discus across the rusting barricade of barbed wire and out over the fields.

Now, without a commander, and aware of the carnage behind him, the driver halted, waiting upon orders that could not come, while the machine gunners on either side of him desperately searched for the anti-tank gun they believed to be in the ruined houses ahead.

Seeing the tank halt, and the obvious damage to the turret, the British Light Infantry who had been following them went to ground.

Seebohn said,

'I shouldn't think there's too much to worry about now.'

Boden snapped,

'Speak for yourself, I've got my arm to worry about. All you've got to worry about is your Iron Cross.'

Having seen what had happened to GREYHOUND,

DERVISH was on the move again, rumbling through the battlefield debris towards Richter's panzer.

The driver and gunners inside GREYHOUND now found themselves in a dark haze of chemical smoke as the wiring started to smoulder, although there was no fire. Blood dripped down from the corpses in the fighting compartment and mixed with hot oil from the engine compartment to give off a sickening smell.

Private Vaughan, the port machine gunner, called out,

'We can't go on like this, chum. The next bull's eye will do the same for us.'

Private Vaughan wasted no more time. Opening the turret hatch above his head he pushed himself through, and, diving for the rear of the starboard track, took cover behind a pile of masonry.

Driver Abbott, however, was still fumbling with the hatch release, unaware that the two pound gun depressed above it would in any case make it impossible to open, when Boden's second shot struck the driver's visor. The impact of this round snapped the rivets of the visored plate which stood away from the glacis between the two machine gun turrets, so that this section of 14 mm steel was carried back into the driver's chest, as the tungsten carbide shot passed through his sternum, collapsing his rib cage into the left ventricle of the heart.

At the exact moment that the shot struck home, Sergeant Stephenson had pulled himself out of the upper hatch above the left hand Vickers machine gun turret, as the brittle armour fractured in splinters, severing the ulna above his right wrist before piercing his abdomen and fracturing his pelvis. In consequence, Sergeant Stephenson collapsed half-way out of his turret hatch like a mangled jack-in-the-box, as his life drained away from his severed artery.

Inside the driver's compartment, the tungsten carbide core of the armour piercing shot separated from the section of steel plate it had sucked into the tank as it had torn into it, and, having passed through the dead driver, slammed into the steel bulkhead behind his seat before rattling like a demented die in a dice box, igniting the service manuals and cleaning scrim, ricocheting backwards and forwards through his body and against the walls. Smoke began to drift out of the shattered driver's visor.

The British Infantry Tank DERVISH was not encouraged by this spectacle, but there was nothing that the Commander could do about it, since the tank relied on the protection of its 60 mm frontal armour and carried no two pounder. He could only order the machine gunner to continue to play his Vickers over the ruined block of houses ahead.

'What do we do now?' Wundshammer asked.

'Chase them off. What else? Put us into reverse and drive carefully, I don't want my arm fractured, it's bad enough as it is.'

In the close confines of the room, the roar of the 140 hp Maybach Engine was deafening as Wundshammer backed out into the overgrown garden once more.

Wundshammer said,

'You made a couple of lucky shots.'

Boden said,

'It got so close, it was impossible to miss. I'm just glad I got them in time.'

'Someone'll have an expensive bill for renovations in that place.'

'I expect they've been waiting to rebuild for twenty years.'

'Maybe we should have done a proper demolition job.'

'I left that to the British.'

Boden felt flushed with victory, and for the moment forgot the painful throbbing in his arm. The same elation had infected Wundshammer. But the only emotion Boden sensed from Seebohn, however, was the apathy of defeat as he sat huddled in his corner.

The Unteroffizier ordered Wundshammer to halt at the end of the wall that joined the back gardens of the terraced houses. As he tracked the horizon through his glasses, he paused as he caught a pin-prick of light in the woods behind Haucourt, and a second later he heard the insistent rush of a low trajectory shell.

'Where now?' Wundshammer asked.

'Stay put. I don't want to make any kind of target with an eighty eight around. Seebohn, shift your arse and make yourself useful, put the flag out across the engine compartment. Make sure it hangs down the back so that any artillery spotters can see who we are. I don't want any accidents at this stage.'

The flag had been put away when they'd refuelled at Croisilles, and nobody had remembered to replace it before they left.

Seebohn did as he was told in silence.

Once he had climbed back, Boden glanced over his shoulder and said appreciatively,

'That certainly gives me more confidence.'

As he spoke, he ducked instinctively, hearing a fresh burst of machine gun fire from the British Infantry Tank, and his arm was wracked with pain once more as it struck the gun mounting.

Boden heard the faint whisper of a second eighty eight shot thirty yards away, and the air surrounding the British Infantry Tank seemed to vibrate as the round impacted just below the turret.

This time there was no shower of sparks or scooped out indentation of steel to indicate that the hit had registered but not penetrated; the Infantry Tank began to disintegrate in slow motion before Boden's eyes as the hard core shot twisted the riveted plates, tearing into them as a lobster pick cracks a carapace. From within the tank the Unteroffizier heard a succession of rising screams, abruptly cut off by the metallic echo of ammunition exploding within the fighting compartment.

Then the driver's hatch opened and a man in light brown overalls and wearing a knitted Balaclava helmet pulled himself out and hobbled in what seemed a state of shock.

Halfway to the barbed wire he turned and flung a Mills Grenade towards the line of burning houses before turning and walking back, his shoulders hunched and his hands in his pockets, until one of the British Infantry pulled him down.

Shortly after he made his escape, an exploding round of .303 machine gun ammunition passed through the engine compartment and punctured the petrol tank which immediately exploded; the force of this internal blast distorting the plates of the rear upper hull armour. Looking, as it were, for a way of escape, the flames advanced forward through the fighting compartment, incinerating the body of the dead British machine gunner.

Seebohn said,

'We've certainly gained a victory.'

Wundshammer said,

'No thanks to you.'

They had not been alone in observing the destruction of the British Infantry Tank, and now Boden caught a sudden ripple of movement in the middle distance that indicated that the British riflemen were now withdrawing.

'Right, Wundshammer. Let's put an end to their troubles, once I've spoken to Richter.'

Richter had moved Number 5 panzer out of its shell hole by the time that Boden's panzer rumbled over.

'There's a signal from the Leutnant. We're to encircle this attack group.'

'That's a tall order without any infantry around.'

'He says we'll just have to do the best we can.'

'All right, but don't let's waste any time, you take the left flank and I'll take the right.' Boden glanced down at the map. 'We'll cut them off at the crossroads beyond La Marliere. I should think that's where they've left their transport.'

'If they've any petrol.'

'Oh, and signal Regiment to inform the SS that it's perfectly safe for them to reoccupy their former position.'

Richter laughed.

'I'll enjoy doing that.'

As Wundshammer made a wide sweep across the fields, Boden hoped that his estimate would prove correct and that La Marliere, the nearest village, was the British start line. Looking north he could see scattered groups of British riflemen, running from hedgerow to hedgerow, across the flat exposed fields, where they took up all round defensive positions against an invisible enemy. Back at Arlcourt he could see that the British Infantry Tank was still burning, sending up a plume of black smoke into the clear blue summer sky.

Wundshammer shifted restlessly in the driver's seat.

'Just look at that,' he said.

They were now crossing a position that had been occupied earlier by a German Company, although it was impossible to tell at that distance whether the defenders had been SS or Wehrmacht. The riflemen occupying it had been either machine gunned or bayoneted, the stomachs of several were ripped open in blood-dried gashes, and their corpses now lay grinning up to the sky, jaws set in the universal and hideous grimace of death. The body of one rifleman, whose legs had been blown off, knelt grotesquely forward as though he was examining the ground for something which he had lost. His helmet was missing and the wind ruffled his fair hair, giving him an illusory semblance of life.

Seebohn said,

'The British will pay for this.'

Boden said,

'Oh they will, will they? You had your chance back in the houses and loused it up. In any case, don't talk too soon; there could be surprises in store.'

The Mark 2 panzer began to cross a potato field that lay at the south west approach to La Marliere. From time to time they passed more corpses, some of them German and some of them British. Boden tried to put away the sickening feeling he had as the panzer rolled past them.

'Keep away from the dead men, Wundshammer, I'm not in the mood.'

Then his pulse began to race as he saw that the road west out of La Marliere was lined with British transport. Telling Wundshammer to stop he traversed until the truck at the extreme end of the line was in his sights.

Two hundred metres away a driver with a tin helmet at the back of his head, and stripped to the waist, had removed the right hand bonnet flap and was checking the engine.

Boden depressed the elevation of the 2 cm gun until it was in alignment with the cylinder block of the Morris three tonner that was last in line.

When he fired, the truck staggered, hovering for a moment on two wheels before overturning across the road as he had intended. Flames now began to flicker over the wooden sides and tailboard and began to consume the canvas canopy. The other trucks presently began to mill wildly about, as the drivers either tried to reverse back into the village or negotiate the embankment at the roadside, to escape into the fields. The only truck that succeeded in doing so was rapidly embedded up to the back axle in soft earth as the two wheel drive vainly sought to gain traction. Boden saw Richter's tank a hundred metres away on the far side of the road and sent up a white success signal before going to meet him.

Boden said from his turret,

'Allow the British to get to the hedge at the edge of that potato field, but if they try and break out to the east don't hesitate to use your MG.'

Richter said,

'We can handle that. You should have your arm seen to.'

'Later. I'll organise things my side of the road.' He glanced at his watch. 'We'll let them sweat it out for ten minutes, and then put them in the bag.'

While he was speaking Boden heard the roar of engines overhead, and glanced up to see a circus of Stukas making their approach to bomb Arras.

Richter said,

'Last in and first out, that's the Luftwaffe for you. If they'd been in here earlier they could have dealt with the British heavies in no time at all.'

Boden said,

'There must have been other problems to sort out.'

Richter shrugged. 'It's been a long day. How's your arm?'

'There's nothing much to it, it's gone stiff now and the pain is just about bearable. I never thought it would happen to me, but there you are. Start bringing them in on your side in ten minutes, all right?'

Richter nodded and shouted to Stossen, acting as driver, to move past the burning line of British Transport onto the far side of the road.

'All right, Wundshammer, let's get back to our potato field.'

As scattered groups of British infantry continued to cross the fields up to the hedge, where they realised they could go no further because of the patrolling panzers, Boden ordered Seebohn to fire a burst at any obvious target. It would not be long before the ditch behind the hedgerow would be a concentration of unprotected infantry. He ordered Wundshammer to drive up and down parallel with the hedge.

'No faster than walking pace, make them feel nervous. They won't have time to dig in properly.'

Boden stood in the turret holding himself steady with the rim of the open hatch with his left hand. He felt exhilarated and curiously unafraid, although he knew that he was a sitting target and that a single well aimed rifle shot could permanently extinguish his feeling of triumph. Watching the hedge, he could see the round helmeted British Infantry crouched to the ground, while only the rumble of the panzer's engine disturbed the silence of the late afternoon.

'First a burst, Seebohn.'

Seebohn did so, and the sound of the dying shots merged with a choking cry as an infantryman leapt to his feet and crashed through the hedgerow, shot through the throat.

'When you're in the middle, stop, Wundshammer. Seebohn, traverse the gun.'

Two minutes later, two men, one of them a Corporal, stepped out of the hedge with their arms raised, having pointedly thrown down their rifles. In a matter of moments they were joined by fifty others, some supporting wounded, all of them silent. Boden saw on their faces something he had not seen before, not the indifference of 'Les Joyeux', but exhaustion, battle fatigue and defeat.

Boden climbed out of the turret, forgetting the pain and ostentatiously waving his machine pistol in his left hand.

'Who is the NCO in charge here?'

The men glanced at each other until finally the Corporal stepped forward.

'I am, Corporal Kelly.'

'You wish to surrender?'

'That is correct.'

'Form your men into a column and see that they deposit their arms and ammunition as they march to the road.'

'What about our wounded?'

'You will detail a medical section to look after the wounded. They will be cared for by our people in the village.'

The Corporal saluted and detailed a Lance Corporal to form the men up. Boden wondered at the simplicity of the whole operation.

Suddenly there was a sharp crack to his left and he heard Seebohn roar in agony as a 2.5 inch Boys anti-tank rifle round struck home and penetrated the turret armour, sending a steel splinter into the Wireless Operator's left shoulder.

Seebohn appeared at the turret immediately, waving his machine pistol,

'Bastards! Filthy, treacherous, British bastards!'

Boden was appalled by Seebohn's loss of control. It seemed he had every intention of mowing the prisoners down.

'Cut that out, Seebohn!'

Seebohn was still covering the prisoners, who were frozen into an awed silence by his menacing manner.

Boden waved his own machine pistol at Seebohn.

'The only massacre I'm having on my hands is yours, and after this afternoon I wouldn't lose much sleep over that.'

Seebohn shouted out angrily,

'Who said anything about taking prisoners, anyway?'

'Because it is cleaner that way and more professional. We're not savages!'

Seebohn lowered his weapon.

'The killing stops when the shooting stops,' Boden went on. 'They've conceded the battle.'

'The battle has not been conceded.'

'Clear off from up there, Seebohn – take over from him, Wundshammer.'

'Yes, Herr Unteroffizier.'

Seebohn's irrational behaviour made Boden particularly angry because it could shift the whole situation against them. If the prisoners thought they were going to be shot anyway they might take preventive measures since they had nothing to lose. It only needed a well placed grenade through the Mark 2's turret hatch to change everything.

Wundshammer took over Seebohn's position in the turret in such a way as to leave him no alternative but to climb down.

'Come over here,' Boden shouted. When Seebohn was beside him, his mouth twitching and his face contorted with rage, Boden went on,

'You're quite right, these prisoners have conceded the battle, which they're entitled to do. But there is still a soldier somewhere out there with an anti-tank rifle who obviously has not. Since you always wanted to be a panzer grenadier, I suggest you go out and look for him.'

Seebohn froze uncertainly.

'Go on, go and get on with it. Go and find him.'

Boden glared angrily at Seebohn, his wounded arm caked with blood.

'Don't add to my troubles. Take your time, I'm sick of the sight of you.'

Boden looked across to the lengthening shadow the late afternoon sun was casting from the hedge.

'We'll probably still be around until it gets dark. You want to live out the past, well, here's your opportunity.'

Seebohn saluted sullenly and then said,

'Very well, Herr Unteroffizier.'

But Boden heard no more shots from the anti-tank rifle as the prisoners were marched down to La Marliere and Seebohn spent the next two hours beating the ditches and occasionally emptying a magazine into the deserted hedgerows to relieve his tormented feelings.

9 Paradise Hotel

As they came to the crossroads at Tilloy, Boden could contain himself no longer.

'Not much of a soldier, are you, Seebohn?'

Seebohn was taken aback by this sudden criticism, as he thought the incident at La Marliere would have been forgotten already, since so many things in war happened so quickly. He had also been annoyed to find that the wound on his left shoulder was only a scratch, whereas it was quite clear from Boden's white face and grim expression that his wound was a good deal more serious.

'I don't know what you mean.'

'Then I'll tell you. You came into our platoon full to the neck with crap about the National Socialists and how wonderful the Brownshirts are, to say nothing of bringing your father's tombstone. Then when things get sticky you disintegrate and, what's more, have the nerve to threaten my prisoners. You're not much fun to be with, Seebohn, even when you're off duty.'

Seebohn wriggled uncomfortably.

'You've no right to say that.'

'I've every right. You're not leading one of your street gangs now, and you can't run off and sneak to your Gauleiter uncle either. You're in the Wehrmacht, with a tradition stretching back to Frederick the Great. We think the S.A. are such crap we won't even bother to acknowledge their existence.'

Seebohn said,

'Talking like that insults the German people. The Army's a bunch of reactionaries. The Party aims to change all that.'

'If the S.A. are all the same as you, a fat chance we'd have ever had of even occupying the Rhineland! I tell you, Seebohn, the first chance I have I'm dumping you, transferring you out and that's a promise. You'd be much happier with your SS friends where you can shit in the corner as hard as you like without any reference to me. Sometimes they use prisoners for target practice, that should be right up your street.'

Seebohn was so overwhelmed by the depth of feeling behind these remarks that he could think of no suitable reply. What made it worse was that he had developed a grudging admiration for the way that the Unteroffizier went about things, and wanted him as a friend, feeling that he could change his political attitude in time. As to what had happened at Arlcourt, he put down his failure to the accumulated stresses of the past week. He naturally did not allow that the rest of the crew had been subjected to equal stress, particularly Boden with his wound.

He still had no wish to back down however.

'That's no way to talk to a National Socialist.'

'Any more of that, Seebohn, and I'll rip off your uniform and leave you by the roadside in your underpants with a French Army dog tag round your neck. Then your SS friends'll bump you off for joining the Foreign Legion and taking up arms against the Fatherland. Laugh that off if you can. I'm not even sure you deserve to wear the panzer uniform anyway.'

Seebohn appealed to Wundshammer.

'What d'you think about it?'

'I'm sorry; I'm a fair minded man but I have to agree with every word he says. You joined us announcing that you intended to win the Iron Cross First Class, but all you've been is a liability with your constant bitching on. I've been driving non-stop ever since the Frontier, and there you sit with damn all else to do sounding off Party slogans. You're a luxury we can't afford, even if your Uncle the Gauleiter reads you *Mein Kampf* every night. Why, you can't even fuck without a machine pistol in one hand!'

Seebohn fell silent, brooding over this frank opinion and straining to think how he could regain favour in some small degree.

At length Wundshammer pulled into the forward panzer

park, where the corrugated Junkers JU 52s stood ranged along the improvised landing strip runway, backlit by the faint glow of the night sky, as shadowy, black overalled Luftwaffe personnel rolled out 500 litre drums of petrol for the panzers.

Boden looked over to Seebohn and said,

'We could do with some petrol.'

Seebohn swallowed and then said to Wundshammer, who by this time had switched off the engine,

'What d'you mean I can't fuck?'

'You're useless at human relations, and you talk to everyone as though they were a captive audience at a Party meeting. Since you're so anxious to wipe out the human race, it's hardly surprising you don't find the girls co-operative.'

Seebohn, like anyone else whose personality is under an adverse microscope, did not want to let the matter drop.

'That's not a comradely way to talk! I get on well with girls.'

'I haven't seen much evidence.'

By this time Boden was thoroughly fed up with Seebohn, and in any case he wanted to get to the Aid Post.

'Just go and get the petrol will you, Seebohn? Your sex life's not such a fascinating topic. Then go and draw a wireless. If I hadn't had to get outside the panzer to talk to Richter, this arm would never have happened.'

Seebohn had enough sense to realise that that was the end of the conversation so far as everyone else was concerned, and so reluctantly climbed out of the panzer to organise the petrol.

Boden said,

'Take a nap while you can, Wundshammer, I'm going to have my arm repaired.'

Boden got treatment at the Aid Post after a certain amount of argument.

'You'll have to go back to the Feld Lazarett at St Quentin.'

'No thanks, I don't want to be invalided out, just have this lump of shrapnel removed.'

'You need a theatre for that.'

'Balls. A pair of forceps and some antiseptic. I'd do it myself, only I'm not left handed.'

The Medical Orderly could see that ultimately it would be simpler to give in and in this way get rid of Boden for good, but he made a last attempt to apply the system. 'You should really go in to X-ray.'

'I really shouldn't be here at all. Do me a favour, Doctor, and just patch me up. You can turn me into a medical experiment after I've got to the Channel.'

'What makes it so urgent?'

'Oh, just a silly kind of competition.'

The Orderly took a probe out of the sterilisation cabinet.

'You're going to hate this. I should really give you a local.'

'Forget the frills, there's no time. I just want it out rather than in.'

Boden winced as the Orderly deftly twisted the forceps round the lump of metal, extracting it from beside the bone.

'Luckily for you there doesn't seem to be any material in the wound and the artery's calmed down. I'll put some coagulant on and a piece of gauze. But when you can find a moment, I suggest you get some stitches in.'

'I haven't got a moment.'

'Then I'll put on a bandage.'

Boden found Leutnant Von Dressen enjoying a bottle of Schnapps beside the Company Commander's Mark 3 panzer and stood to attention in place of a salute.

'Good evening, Boden. From the reports I've had you seem to have redeemed yourself.'

Boden noticed that Von Dressen's tunic was torn and his eyes were red with fatigue.

'Were there any more British, Herr Leutnant?'

'Quite a few, the Divisional Commander's never been so worried since half the panzers broke down halfway to Vienna. Anyway, we held the British to get the eighty eights into position, which was the whole idea. The Mark 3s are mopping up in front of Beaurains.'

'Many losses?'

'Just one or two mediums. As you know their Cruisers were armed with quite an impressive two pounder.'

'Can we expect more trouble?'

'Not that I know of. The BEF only had an Armoured Brigade and some obsolete light tanks for a start. Now we're at Doullens they'll be running out of petrol.'

Boden nodded towards the Junker JU 52 that was revving up its three engines before take off.

'Unlike us?'

'As you say. Anyway, I don't think it can go on much longer. The British are pulling back to what's left of the Channel ports, and once we get to Abbéville they'll be sealed in a pocket. We'll be able to do what we like with them.'

'I'm rather afraid of that happening.'

'Oh? Has Seebohn been threatening to put his theories into practice?'

'He's not had the chance.'

'The trouble is, he believes all the propaganda.'

'Don't we know it; he'd be much more useful carrying a flag or organising a rally somewhere nice and safe behind the line.'

'Like that, is it? Oh well, you can't tell how someone will react. Take Haagen and Loeker; when they were hit Loeker wanted to stay behind to put out a petrol fire, he said if they didn't have transport they'd never make Calais. Haagen had to drag him away.'

'I'd not heard that story.'

'The French put in a sketchy appearance to the south and fired off some guns. Number 4 panzer got in the way of a 7.5.'

'Then Redwitz is out of the race?'

'I wouldn't count on it. They've rustled up a BMW motorbike combination from somewhere and call themselves advance reconnaissance troops. They seem to have every intention of being first to the Channel.'

Von Dressen offered Boden the Schnapps bottle which he refused, and an Eckstein which he accepted.

'What do you want me to do now?'

'Get your panzer checked out. From what I hear, it needs a service.'

'Richter wants to hit the road right away once we've refuelled.'

'That's up to him. My orders are to cut across north to Calais. I'm not stopping anyone from going anywhere at this stage of the campaign. Who gets there first is between you three.'

Boden put out his cigarette, since he found it awkward to smoke with his left hand, and thanked the Leutnant, who said,

'Don't do anything silly; the war's not over yet.'

'I don't intend to, Herr Leutnant.'

Boden walked back to his panzer and was surprised to find that Seebohn, having finished re-fuelling, was now feverishly at work installing the new wireless set he had just drawn from Stores.

'What are you doing, Seebohn?'

'There aren't any machinists available so I thought I would get on and do it myself. How's your arm?'

'Will it work?'

'I'll see that it does.'

For a moment Boden speculated on Seebohn's sudden desire to please before he realised he didn't care.

Boden found Redwitz and his newly acquired BMW beside Richter's panzer.

'Hullo, joined the Storm grenadiers?'

'We had a lucky break and found this motorbike after Recovery took away our panzer. We'll be racing along the pave at a hundred kmh.'

'Provided there isn't any opposition.'

'I was talking to a Corporal in the air recce unit and there's not much danger of that. The whole front's breaking. The French Armoured Divisions to the north are out of fuel and the British are streaming back to the coast.'

'Still,' said Boden, 'there's always room for the unexpected.'

Richter joined them, looking pleased with himself.

'Your wireless operator, Seebohn, certainly knows the score.'

'Why? What's he done now?'

'He's got hold of the address of an establishment in Arras. If you know the sort I mean.'

Boden said,

'I don't believe it. I just don't believe it.'

'It's true. I checked it out.'

'Anyway it can't be in business any more, the way Arras has been flattened.'

'Ah but this rest centre is tucked away on the outskirts, a place called Paradise Hotel. You know how expert the French are supposed to be when it comes to organising that kind of thing. The Intelligence Sergeant confirmed everything and advised us to get it in first before the officers grabbed it and made it out of bounds.'

Wundshammer said,

'I never thought that Seebohn knew places like that even existed.'

'It's odd he hasn't mentioned it to you,' Haagen said to Boden.

'We're not exactly blood brothers.'

'He thinks we should look in on the way north.'

Boden noticed Loeker wink at Redwitz.

'It's perfectly O.K. by me so long as we all have an evening out. I reckon we deserve it. I intend to see Paris as well, of course.'

Haagen laughed.

'Of course, don't we all?'

At nine o'clock that night, 6 Platoon set off in convoy along the blacked out road from Tilloy, before being diverted north from the smouldering centre of Arras by the Feldgendarmerie signs into the Boulevard de la Scarpe; crossing the river by the pioneer bridge before branching left at the Rue de Lens to take the Calais Road.

Boden had not spoken to Seebohn since Tilloy and therefore the question of the Paradise Hotel had not been raised. Seebohn sat glued to his new wireless set, fiddling with the frequency dial and trying to find a music programme.

Then he said abruptly,

'I've heard of a place round here.'

'A place, Seebohn? What sort of place?'

'A place where we can all put our feet up for an hour or two. Enjoy female company.'

'I thought that sort of thing didn't interest you?'

'That's an impression I've every intention of correcting.'

'Oh? And where is this Nirvana? Buried under the ruins we've just by passed?'

'No, it's in the Avenue Chatte. In fact it's in this neighbourhood along the Rue de Lens.'

'It sounds irregular to me. I don't know how you came to think of such a thing.'

'It's somewhere off this road. We'll come to it any moment.'

'Oh all right, Seebohn, if it's that important to you. But I expect you'll find it empty. They'll have pushed off like all the others.'

After five minutes of silence, Seebohn, who had been keeping an anxious look out, told Wundshammer to slow down.

'It'll be the next turning left, the one after Rue des Capucins. There, Avenue Chatte.'

Wundshammer turned down a dark and deserted street lined with detached villas. Halfway down, the Mark 2's headlamp beam picked out a flaking sign: PARADISE HOTEL. ACCOMMODATION. FIRST CLASS ROOMS.

'That's it, that's it!' Seebohn called out.

Wundshammer said,

'There's nothing I can see to get excited about.'

'Girls, girls,' Seebohn shouted. 'We all want girls!'

'That rather depends what the girls are like,' Wundshammer said.

As Richter's panzer drew up behind them, closely followed by Haagen, Loeker and Redwitz on their motorbike combination, Boden said,

'Well, it was your idea, Seebohn. You better go and knock them up.'

Boden's arm ached and suddenly he felt tired. He didn't really know why he had agreed to Seebohn's proposal, except out of curiosity, since it was so out of character. The fact that Seebohn wanted to be accepted was in itself a new development. So far as the afternoon's battle was concerned, his mind was a blank. All he wanted now was a decent meal and some sleep. He could not face the goulash and noodles that had been available at the field kitchen, and the coffee had been ersatz. He tried to work out when he had last eaten.

'All right,' Boden said. 'Make this a night that everyone will remember, Seebohn, and I'll forget what a bastard you are. I might even forget about everything.'

When he closed his eyes he had the visual image of the dead English Sergeant hanging half out of the Cruiser Tank. No sooner had he flopped down in a stream of blood across the rivets of the dark green glacis plate than the flies had descended. Whatever side they were on, the end was the same. He only hoped he wouldn't go like that.

He watched Seebohn go to the door and tug the antiquated bell pull. Now he could see that there was a faint glimmer behind the curtain of the first floor window. For what seemed the hundredth time that day, Boden heaved himself clumsily out of the turret hatch and walked under the peach tree in the garden to where Seebohn was waiting. Then the door was opened by a woman in a dressing gown.

'Monsieur?'

Seebohn, taken aback by this informal reception, tried to make the best of it.

'We are German Army. Have you Champagne? We will pay.'

'British, French, German Army, what difference does it make? So long as the money is good.'

Seebohn stammered,

'There are eight of us.'

'Don't worry, there is plenty of Champagne.'

Boden stepped inside as the woman held the door open, to find the hall lit by an oil lamp. It looked like a back street hotel in any provincial town. Advertisements for DUBON-

NET and STELLA ARTOIS had been stuck to the wall next to a poster for the 1939 New York World Fair. Underneath were pinned a string of garish post cards from Marseilles, Cannes and Nice.

'We have had no electricity for two days and the taps don't work any more, but there is a well in the garden.'

Seebohn said stiffly,

'It is a time of emergencies.'

By now the rest of the panzer crews had come inside and Haagen, Redwitz and Loeker hung up their long motorcycle coats next to the reception desk, laying their machine pistols on the shelf above.

The woman stared at their black uniforms and then asked Seebohn:

'What is this uniform? Are you parachutists or sailors?'

'No, this is the German panzer uniform.'

'Ah, German panzers. You must be officers. Before there were some British but they were very formal.'

Seebohn tried his hand at a joke.

'I don't know any personally.'

'Of course not. How could you? Now, I shall have one of my girls bring you Champagne. It is very good. Premier Cru. That means it is First Choice. My cousin works for a shipper at Epernay, so I only stock the best at a very advantageous price.'

The panzer crew lay back in the armchairs that lined the walls of the large room opening out beyond the reception desk. Richter lit a cigarette.

'What kind of a place did you say this is?' he asked Seebohn. 'It's a clip joint, drink and dancing. Someone's been having you on.'

Presently the woman performing the role of manageress returned, accompanied by a girl with blonde hair dark at the roots. She wore a blouse that revealed a generous cleavage, and a gold cross dangled between her breasts.

'This is Mathilde. She will make you feel at home. But first there is the question of the bill. Here, when you book a room, you must pay in advance. It will be nine hundred francs altogether, but that includes the dinner and local taxes, with all the other services.'

Seebohn who was out of his depth looked around helplessly.

'Nine hundred francs?'

Boden said,

'About ninety Deutschmarks.'

The Manageress smiled and wrinkled her calculating eyes.

'Afterwards there will be dancing and you can escort the girls; we have a gramophone and Maurice Chevalier records. Nine hundred francs and the cost of the Champagne. I promise you, you won't regret it.'

Boden said,

'All right, Seebohn, this is on your fat uncle the Gauleiter.'

For a moment it seemed that Seebohn was going to argue, but then he thought better of it. He pulled his paybook out of the appalling denim trousers he had looted and carefully counted out the money.

'Well done Seebohn. What's on the menu? I'm starving.'

'Because times are difficult it will be simple; soup, crudités, a little salad, a pork chop, some Brie, fruit.'

'That sounds fine,' said Boden. 'Much better than the Goulash Cannon.'

'Maybe I was wrong, maybe Seebohn picked a winner after all,' Richter commented.

'Not bad,' said Haagen. 'I'd like to have something to compare with Paris.'

'You'll end up in the Rhine, you can't even read a map,' Wundshammer said.

They all laughed at that as Mathilde returned to spread a red and white check cloth over the long table at one side of the room.

Richter, on his third glass of Champagne, asked,

'Do you speak German?'

Mathilde smiled and shook her head.

'Who cares, love is the international language.'

Boden could hear the steady throb of the panzers in the distance as they moved north through the night to Béthune.

He still felt tired and his arm ached; when he shut his eyes still all he could see was burning tanks.

Nobody could quarrel with the food after a week of irregular field kitchen rations. As the evening wore on, Seebohn began to expand. He kept on telling them the most stupid jokes at which they felt obliged to laugh since he was paying; but he kept off politics.

Finally he announced,

'The war is over, and so it is time to cement the peace.'

Glancing at him, Boden realised that he was drunk. The Wireless Operator went on,

'I wish to drink to the Panzer Platoon of which I have the honour to be a member, also to our Company Commander with his ridiculous monocle and Leutnant Von Dressen who cannot be with us here tonight, since we have placed this establishment out of bounds to Officers. Prosit.'

Richter said,

'I'll drink to that.'

They all laughed again, knowing that Richter had fallen foul of the Leutnant at Trier where he had been accused of commanding a filthy panzer simply because an engine gland had leaked a spot of oil during Regimental Inspection.

Mathilde, having removed the debris from the table, now returned with three other girls. One of them put a record on the gramophone.

Haagen shouted,

'Why don't you tune in to Radio Stuttgart, they transmit all the best dance bands.'

Pauline, the dark haired girl, said,

'That's easy, our set's got flat batteries. Anyway who wants to hear the news? Like someone said, it's all over.'

'Don't blame your Army, it's your Generals who didn't know what they were doing.'

'Yours certainly seem to.'

The Tunisian girl who wore a yellow flower in her hair put on a record that Boden remembered hearing last Christmas. The incommunicable tensions of the war were somehow underlined by the empty, conventional lyrics.

'Boom – Why did my heart go Boom?

Why did my heart go Boom-Boomity Boom?
Because I love you.'

The French tenor's words merged into the swish of the rhythm brushes and the wailing throb of the saxophones. When it had finished, the last girl, Marie, who had red hair and blue eyes, put it on again. Her skirt fell below her knee and she wore a bolero, long earrings and an almost invisible chain round her ankle.

Bending down to wind up the gramophone and operate the control, she leaned against Boden and he caught the perfume of her body. She noticed his reaction and said,

'Hello German soldier.'

'What's your name?'

'Marie Blanche. What's yours?'

'Micki.'

'What happened to your poor arm, Micki?'

In spite of himself, Boden responded to her concern, although he knew it was more apparent than real.

'Oh, that. It was a grenade splinter. Nothing serious.'

At the same time a thrill of passion passed through Boden's solar plexus, partly induced by the perfume and partly by her proximity.

Looking at her more closely he could read a sullen defiance in her face, as though she had already experienced most of the things, good and bad, that life had to offer and she really didn't care any more.

'Would you like to dance?'

'If your arm's all right.'

Boden held her gently with his good arm, sliding into the quickstep rhythm of the record.

'That's nice. You dance well, I thought you Germans would be all footstamping, lederhosen and Adolf Hitler.'

Boden was irritated by this comment and said,

'Why is it that we're always thought of as savages?'

A moment later he felt her nibbling at his ear.

'Don't worry, darling. I do it for free anyway, especially for someone who's tall, dark and handsome and wearing a black uniform. Who knows, it could be your last time, so I'd want to give you the happiest memories.'

Boden now became aware that Seebohn and Wundshammer were arguing over the girl with the yellow flower, who was sitting between them on the settee. Wundshammer said,

'Of course Valerie likes you, even if you are wearing looted trousers that are two sizes too small.'

Valerie said,

'Be quiet you two boys. I want to hear about the panzer battle.'

Seebohn said,

'I saw it all. I was in the turret most of the time, until the final attack came. I had to act as gunner because no-one else was able.'

Wundshammer said:

'Don't listen to him, darling. He couldn't even load the gun, let alone fire it.' Then he kissed her on the neck.

'You're not going to get away with that, Wundshammer, there's a story or two I could tell about you!'

'Not interested. I've nothing on my conscience, which is why I can do things like this.'

Wundshammer put his arm round Valerie and drew her onto his knee.

'I was talking about your driving.'

'What do you think of it, Valerie?'

The Tunisian girl showed her teeth and laughed. 'In any case,' Wundshammer went on, starting to massage the top of Valerie's thigh. 'Everyone knows about the General's half track.'

'What happened?' Valerie asked with little girl, wide open eyes.

'It's not important. We're the only two people who are important.' Wundshammer kissed Valerie's breasts.

'That wasn't the accident I meant,' Seebohn said viciously. 'No, not that one at all. I meant the time you ran down Buchser.'

Wundshammer had shut his eyes as a gesture that he couldn't be bothered to listen to Seebohn's irrelevant and jealous ramblings. Now he opened them again.

'Ran down Buchser? Jesus Christ, what the hell do you mean by that?'

'Don't tell me you didn't know?'

'Shit,' said Wundshammer. 'Shit! So that was it.' He sank back into the settee cushions and covered his face with his hands. Then he pushed Valerie gently off his knee.

'Excuse me, sweetheart, suddenly I'm not in the mood any more.' Getting up and going over to the table he poured himself a glass of brandy from the half full bottle standing there, then he went off to the shadows of the reception desk.

Valerie looked at Seebohn with dislike.

'You upset him deliberately.'

'Not at all, it was just something that happened. Look, let's have a dance and then go upstairs. I'll tell you how I won the Battle of Arras in my Panzer Mark 2.'

Valerie looked into Seebohn's face and didn't seem to like what she found there.

'No thanks, sweetheart.'

She got up and walked over to where Wundshammer was brooding with a second full glass of brandy. Although Wundshammer didn't take any notice of her, since he was occupied with his own internal heart searchings, Valerie continued to stroke his arm and offer other little affectionate gestures, but nevertheless couldn't persuade him to dance.

Boden had followed every detail of the quarrel between Seebohn and Wundshammer. He was so angry with the wireless operator he would have been quite willing to knock him down, but this would, of course, have only humiliated Wundshammer still more and possibly undermined the discipline of the whole panzer platoon.

Marie Blanche said speculatively, 'I didn't realise you'd been in a battle.'

'Some of us were.'

Marie Blanche realised that there was something wrong and decided to change the subject.

'Well then, how about it?'

'How about what?'

'Why, a little bit of love, of course.'

In the upstairs bedroom Blanche lay down on the divan without bothering to take off her clothes. Then she inched up her skirt slowly until she had revealed a tuft of brown pubic hair.

'It's too warm to put on underwear this weather. I never bother in the summer and when I'm going out. You only have to take them off.'

Then she watched Boden's expression as she slowly opened her legs, until her thighs were open and inviting.

'There, take a good look at the most fascinating sight in the world and pour me a drink, darling.'

Boden felt the passion surge up inside him as he took his time easing off his tunic. His arm still throbbed but he did not notice any pain.

Marie Blanche took the glass he handed her.

'So you've been in action?'

'There was a battle and we took Arras.'

'How funny. I was talking to a British Sergeant the other night. He liked me a lot – called me Mademoiselle from Armentieres. He said I could do it better than anyone he'd ever met, so I must have given him something to remember.'

Boden stood transfixed as the gruesome possibility began to dawn on him.

'As a matter of fact he was the last little friend who played with me. They give their tanks names you know, like race horses, and his was called "Greyhound" or something. He had a family in England.'

Boden sat down on the edge of the bed, suddenly cold all over.

'Well come on, darling, aren't you going to take the dog for a walk? I saw his tank once; they're quite different from your German panzers, I expect.'

'Yes, they're quite different.'

Boden got up slowly and began to put his tunic back on again.

'Don't say you've changed your mind, just after you've got me all worked up?'

'I'm sorry, it's my arm. I'm really under Doctor's orders. I wouldn't be up to it.'

'I could turn over and you could fuck me from the back if that would help.'

'You did say his tank was called Greyhound?'

'Yes, he once told me it's a sort of English sporting dog. I wonder what happened to him. Wouldn't it be funny if you'd actually fired at each other. Of course, he may be dead for all I know.'

Boden said,

'Look, I'd hate you to miss out on having a bit of fun. Come downstairs and I'll introduce you to another sleeping partner.'

'But I want you, baby. I hope there's nothing wrong.'

She looked at him suspiciously.

'Nothing at all.'

'Oh well, why not? It's all the same in the dark.'

She got up, adjusted her skirt and followed the Unteroffizier downstairs. Everyone had disappeared, including Wundshammer and Valerie, but Seebohn was still sitting self-consciously on the settee drinking by himself.

Boden went up to him;

'What's eating you, Seebohn? Can't you find a girl?'

'I don't have to try that hard.'

'I thought you wanted to let down your hair.'

'As a matter of fact I've had a lot to drink.'

'It's the best way of sobering up I've yet discovered. Marie Blanche will tell you that.'

Marie Blanche giggled.

'What's the matter? Doesn't the little boy want to, or is he one of those?'

'What does she mean?'

'Forget it, Seebohn.'

'D'you like going to the Folies Bergere?' Marie Blanche asked. She picked up the hem of her skirt and whisked it to and fro to reveal her stocking tops and fanny.

'That's what they all go to see. Don't you like it?'

Seebohn said,

'Of course I like it.'

'You don't sound too sure. You men are so funny, you always carry dirty pictures around, but when it comes to the real thing you seem to get scared.'

'Is that a proposition?' Seebohn asked.

'Of course it's a proposition. Come on, sweetheart.' Marie Blanche pulled Seebohn to his feet, just when Redwitz, Haagen and Loeker came down the stairs.

'Have fun?' Boden asked.

Haagen replied,

'You bet, these French girls certainly know their stuff, they leave nothing to the imagination.'

Redwitz added,

'After that piece of heaven I'll never lay a Fraulein again, all they do is flop on their backs wearing a pained expression and clenching their fists.'

Boden said,

'Seebohn's just going to find that out for himself.'

As Seebohn and Marie Blanche went upstairs, Haagen called out,

'You'll love it! Once you get going you'll never be able to stop. They don't teach things like that in the Hitler Youth.'

Loeker shouted,

'Stay as long as you like – all night if you want to!'

When they had disappeared the motorcyclists began to put on their long, heavy raincoats.

'I feel better for that,' Haagen said. 'It's really set me up.'

Boden said,

'I'm glad to hear it. Where are you off to now?'

'There's no point in hanging about here, and anyway you've as good as lost the great Channel race as it is. Once Seebohn gets his first bite of the cherry you'll never be able to drag him away.'

'Why should I? He deserves every minute of it.'

'Well we mustn't miss the boat train.'

Boden shrugged and smiled and they went out laughing.

The Unteroffizier now remembered that he had left his panzer beret in Marie Blanche's bedroom so he went upstairs and pushed open the door.

Marie Blanche lay on her back in apparent ecstasy, her knees bent up so that her legs were parallel with the divan. Seebohn had stripped himself in such haste that he hadn't bothered to remove his shirt, working away inside Blanche's thighs like a mad thing. While all this was going on, Blanche from time to time stretched out her nail varnished fingers to take a puff from her cigarette. Then she would open her eyes and blow the smoke in Seebohn's face.

The third time this happened Seebohn suddenly got excited and ripped away her blouse to get at her tits, which spilled out towards each armpit. His passion increased when he found that Marie Blanche had decorated her nipples, which were now erect, with lipstick.

'What the hell do you want?' she shouted to Boden. 'We don't go in for any dirty North African tricks in this house, if a threesome's what you've got in mind!'

Boden said,

'Don't worry. I just looked in to see that you two were getting along all right together.'

'What he lacks in technique he makes up for with enthusiasm.'

'He's a talented boy, his great ambition is to win the Iron Cross.'

'He can have the Grand Prix Fucking Award any day from me.'

Boden picked up his panzer beret and closed the bedroom door behind him.

'Have a good time, you deserve each other.'

10 Nord

Wundshammer was in a depressed state as they rolled along Route Nationale 43 through Bethune the next morning, in contrast to Seebohn who obviously felt very pleased with himself. This did not improve the driver's mood as he turned to where Seebohn was working immediately behind his seat and said,

'Do you mind removing yourself to the far end of the panzer? You smell of cunt.'

Seebohn seemed to accept the criticism as a compliment to his manhood as Wundshammer appealed to Boden,

'Can't we put him out to air? It's getting quite septic in here so I can't concentrate on avoiding the bomb craters. Can't he get outside and fix the aerial or something?'

Boden looked over to Seebohn and asked,

'D'you think you can manage to do that? And when you've finished we'd be happier if you could sit outside and keep an eye open for the RAF.'

Seebohn left the fighting compartment convinced that these remarks confirmed his standing as a lover. When he had gone, Wundshammer said,

'Now he's out of the way, I can tell you that I had a lousy evening.'

'You mean that business about Buchser?'

'Not so much that. It was a bit of a shock, but really when I thought about it, I couldn't accept the blame. I couldn't even hear a shell explode the time that it happened.'

'I'm glad you took it like that. I would say it was an accident of war.'

'What upset me more than anything was the way the bastard Seebohn let it drop. Quite clearly he was upset by the way I was getting along with the Tunisian, and was trying to break it up. Which he succeeded in doing.'

'So you had a lonely evening?'

'Not exactly. After a bit I pulled myself together and got off with Mathilde; that really proved to be uphill work and a bad idea generally.'

'How do you mean?'

'To begin with, the little bourgeoise insisted on filling me in on her life story. Apparently she was married to a village postman near Evreux, but once he'd been mobilised he'd forgotten to send any money, so she ended up on the game. She kept rabbiting on about Evreux's social structure, and I wondered when, if ever, we were going to get down to business. When at last it happened at 2 a.m. she couldn't wait to see me pull it out. "Have you come? Have you come?" she kept on asking, as though it was some kind of race against time and there was another customer waiting. I hope to God I didn't catch a dose; she's the sort that's most likely to pass it on.'

Boden said,

'I can relieve your mind on that score, that's one thing the French administer efficiently. If they didn't they'd have an epidemic on their hands.'

Wundshammer asked,

'How did you get on?'

They had now come to a length of road running through two fields of spring wheat, neatly lined by regular craters. Here, the roadside was littered with abandoned British equipment; burnt out three tonners, fifteen hundred weight trucks together with a scattering of French civilian cars, their roof rack luggage pathetically entwined with branches as a crude attempt at camouflage. The clothes of the corpses surrounding them fluttered in the breeze.

Boden finally answered Wundshammer's question.

'How did I get on? It could have been worse.'

'What? Didn't you get it in?'

'Not likely. That Marie Blanche turned out to be dead man's meat. She'd last been with that British Sergeant in that Cruiser we shot up yesterday.'

Wundshammer gave a long whistle of amazement.

'She told you that?'

'Yes, and identified the name of the tank while she was

removing her drawers, which was why I believed her. That news really brought me up short and dampened my ardour. In the end I handed her on to Seebohn, in the light of everything that had happened. Besides he didn't seem to be having much success with the other girls.'

Wundshammer began to roar with laughter, so much so that he almost crashed into the back of a burned out British ambulance that was slewed across the road.

'You dirty bastard, Boden.'

'I don't see why. If she hadn't told me about the British Sergeant I would probably have had her. So far as I know she didn't tell Seebohn, who seems none the worse for it. Probably it wouldn't have made any difference if she had.'

'I don't suppose he'll jump over the moon if he finds out. He might even think he's been slipped the Ace of Spades.'

'He can think what he likes, I'm not superstitious. Anyway, the experience seems to have improved him and brought out his sunny disposition.'

Wundshammer said,

'He'll more than likely cost us that trip to Paris. Those mad bastards on the BMW are probably sunbathing by this time.'

Boden shrugged.

'You should've seen enough of the Blitzkrieg to realise that anything can happen and probably will.'

Wundshammer changed down at the next crossroads, which had been under shellfire. A British BSA/Daimler Scout Car had received a direct hit and all that now remained was its burned out chassis and fire-blackened upper armour lying side on in the ditch.

The driver had been killed by blast, and his unmarked body had been thrown under a hawthorn thicket, where he was now lying crouched in an irrelevant attitude of death, minutely examining the toecap of his right boot, his khaki beret still perfectly in position. As they drove by Boden could see the flies crawling over his cheeks and into his ears and nostrils.

'God, how I hate flies.'

'At least when we're moving they can't settle.'

Boden now wished that he had exchanged the pleasures of the Paradise Hotel for eight hours of uninterrupted sleep. He realised that he was drained as much by the concentrated experiences of the last ten days as by emotional stress. Everything that had happened seemed crammed into a solid lump of memory, which, taken as a whole, was too concentrated to have meaning, and would only be absorbed if each individual episode was examined separately.

He heard the side tone crackle in his headset.

'Boden?'

'Yes, Herr Leutnant?'

'Where've you got to?'

'Just past Bethune. If we take the main road we'll be about fifty kilometres from Calais.'

'Well it looks like the British are putting everything they've got into the defence of Calais. There are orders to hold out to the last man.'

Boden said,

'We've heard stories like that all the way from the French Frontier, but the last man always seems to have vanished by the time we get there.'

'Well, don't count on it this time. They've sent in three of their better infantry regiments and imported more armour.'

'They won't get far against the Mark 3s.'

'The Mark 3s may not be up in time. There may be a Führer order to all troops to hold their position to allow consolidation.'

'So everyone goes into cold storage?'

'That's right. The Staff are worried about supply and what happened at Arras. If the British had broken through, they could have taken over control of the battle.'

'When do we have to stop?'

'I'll tell you soon enough. Oh, and by the way, the Three Musketeers, Redwitz, Haagen and Loeker have just been roped in to guard some British POWs down the road. You better look out for them, west of Lillers.'

As Von Dressen went off the air, Wundshammer could hardly control his laughter.

'We've had some of that. We know what it's like to be detailed for special assignment. It'll make a change to see their ears burning.'

Wundshammer continued to drive on through battlefield litter and at one point they passed the smashed remains of a Fairey Battle, its camouflaged tailplane pointing skywards and its buckled nose buried in a field of maize.

Seebohn made his way back into the turret and shouted,

'That's the first RAF plane I've seen since the Meuse.'

Wundshammer wrinkled his nose and said,

'Kindly keep downwind, Seebohn.'

'I'm getting sick of that joke.'

'Not as much as I'm getting sick of that cheap perfume you insist on wearing, it reminds me of the dreary tart I had last night.'

'As a matter of fact I rather like it.'

'That's quite obvious; but that doesn't mean to say we have to.'

In fact, Seebohn knew that he was being got at, but didn't really mind, particularly as he noticed that Wundshammer, while not exactly warm, no longer projected hostility, so it seemed that last night's disagreement was now forgotten.

'You seem to have enjoyed yourself last night,' Boden said.

'You can say that again.'

The panzer rolled on along the Lillers road with Richter tagging on behind. Boden found it hard to face the possibility of yet another battle at the end of the road at Calais. Presently, they came to Reincourt les Tilleuls, a hamlet of red brick cottages backing onto a colliery. Beyond the village they arrived at a crossroads with two dirt tracks leading off nowhere. This intersection was marked by a tall stone Calvary, from the steps of which a feldgendarme was directing traffic.

Boden ordered Wundshammer to stop, bending down to shout to the policeman,

'Where's the POW cage?'

The feldgendarme pointed to the left hand track.

'Thanks, Sergeant.'

'Where the hell d'you think you're going?'

'It's all right, Sergeant, we've got to collect our Officer, an English Regiment's surrendered at Les Cajoules and we've been sent to pick him up.'

It was hard to tell whether the feldgendarme followed this story, let alone believed it, but at that moment his attention was diverted by a half tracked mobile panzer gantry, its right hand indicator arm swinging up and down as it followed a sign to an advanced workshop down the opposite track. Its arrival allowed Boden to take the opportunity of making off in the direction of the POW cage. The track took them through a field past a deserted coal depot where sheep were grazing.

Seebohn shouted out,

'Target, left, three hundred. British panzer.'

Boden's heart missed a beat, but when he stared across the field he heard Seebohn laughing.

'Correction. Abandoned British panzer.'

'Just don't do things like that, Seebohn, my nerves can't stand it!'

As they came closer it was clear that the British Mark VIA Light Tank had been abandoned, since all the hatches had been flung wide open.

After five hundred metres they came to the POW cage which consisted of a field in which two hundred men were huddled. Boden looked at the prisoners more closely; they wore English battledress, except for a dozen or so cooks in white overalls. They were a typical unattached 'B' echelon assortment of drivers, linesmen, clerks and machinists.

Haagen was standing at the gate, viciously twisting his machine pistol. He looked up as he heard the rumble of Boden's panzer. As Boden got out Haagen tried, not very successfully, to disguise his annoyance.

'I wondered when you'd hear the news and show up, Herr Unteroffizier.'

'What happened to you, then?'

'Very funny. We've been roped in for this little job. The bastards down the road took our bike at gunpoint and said we'd stolen it. Now they use it to put in appearance at "Appel".'

'Looks like you're stuck here then.'

'That's right, for the duration. What makes it worse is that they've searched the prisoners and removed anything worth having. Loeker and Redwitz have filled in time going through their pockets again and came up with nothing. We're marooned here until we can get hold of some transport and start to catch up with the front.'

'You have my sympathy.'

'These buggers demand more than that. All they ask for is when the Goulash Cannon's coming or try and bum our cigarettes, apart from getting permission to go and crap in the bushes. It's not what I'd planned at all.'

'Why don't you shove off and join the infantry? I don't suppose they'd even notice that you'd gone.'

'Those whining Swiss-Deutsch at the crossroads would all right. They know they've got us by the short and curlies.'

'Love will find a way.'

'Thanks a lot, but if you're thinking of being in first for a paddle, I should glance over your shoulder and ask yourself where Richter's buggered off to.'

In spite of himself, Boden looked round uncomfortably. He'd forgotten about Richter, who'd obviously decided he preferred to stick to the main road.

'Another thing. If you've waltzed down this track without the feldgendarme's O.K. I can tell you you're in big trouble. He'll be the first to grab your panzer and keep you down here to help.'

'Thanks for the tip. What happens further down this track?'

'God knows. We left our maps in the saddlebags. There seem to be some buildings beyond those trees.'

'I think I'll find my way out by the backdoor then. At least the road's heading in the right direction. I can smell the sea.'

'But what about us, Herr Unteroffizier? You can't throw us to the feldgendarmerie, we'll end up in a Penal Battalion.'

'Look,' said Boden, 'the remedy's in your hands. Coming

down the road we spotted an English panzer that's probably only out of gas. In that field back there.'

'Christ, that's a brainwave,' said Haagen. 'Look, lend us your swastika flag and a couple of cans of petrol and we're on our way back. I'm sick of the sight of arseholes straining away in the undergrowth.'

'Yes, and paint on the black and white cross, first chance you have.'

By this time Haagen was almost smiling.

'You better not give me too many tips or we might even catch up. It's more than likely those British Mark VIs are designed for speed, though the armour's probably like paper.'

Seebohn handed over two full jerricans and their red, white and black flag with a furtive air as though he was involving himself in some criminal transaction.

'Relax, Seebohn,' Haagen said, 'think of last night. Could anything have been better?'

On previous form this would have been just the cue for Seebohn to come out with some self-righteous comment about the doubtful legality of disposing of German Army property without authorisation. However, he didn't say anything about that.

'I'm still thinking about her. She had tits like melons.'

'The memory of Marie Blanche will keep you going till next time.'

'I can't wait for that to happen.'

Boden looked incredulously at Seebohn, since he had difficulty in believing that the wireless operator's recent sexual experience could have effected such a striking change. When he came to think about it, Seebohn had been more than usually co-operative so far that morning.

He waved to Haagen, who had now been joined by Loeker and Redwitz.

'O.K., I'll send you a post card from Calais.' When he looked back he saw them running across to the abandoned British Light Tank with its curious beetle-like profile, spoked wheel suspension and set back turret.

'Why do you have to do them favours, after the casual

way they pushed off last night?' Wundshammer asked.

'I'm not letting the feldgendarmerie get away with it, for one thing. I'd like to see that Sergeant's face, next time he drives down to watch "Appel".'

'Don't worry,' Wundshammer said. 'Those Kriegies aren't going anywhere. All they want is to be added to the ration strength while waiting for the Red Cross parcels to drop through the letter box.'

'How can you tell?' Boden asked.

'It's obvious. If any of them really wanted to push off it wouldn't be particularly difficult now, would it, if they really tried, especially since Haagen has obviously lost all interest in the proceedings. A half hearted burst with his machine pistol and that would be all, if he even bothered to make the gesture.'

'I thought they were ordered to escape,' Seebohn said.

Wundshammer laughed.

'They look like civilians in uniform, not soldiers. They'd be much happier in a garage or kneading dough in a bakery.'

The Mark 2 panzer was now ploughing westwards between the overgrown hedgerows lining the narrow lane.

Boden looked back at the top of the hill to see the British Tank, toylike at that distance, draped with the Swastika flag hurrying down the reverse slope of the hill they had just crossed.

'A fast moving job,' Seebohn commented.

'Don't worry, two jerricans won't take him very far. He's going to have to find a petrol point.'

Wundshammer said,

'We seem to be coming up to those houses.'

'Does it look as though we're running out of road?'

'To be quite honest, it doesn't seem too hopeful.'

The track petered out at a farmyard surrounded by outhouses, and Seebohn jumped down and began to wander about, forcing the locked doors.

'For God's sake don't stop a bullet at this stage of the game,' Boden called out. 'There could be a sniper.'

Seebohn smiled, one of the few times the Unteroffizier

could remember such a unique event.

The Wireless Operator continued to inspect the farm buildings, poking about the stables, the empty milking shed and the barns.

'What's he after?' Wundshammer asked. 'Is he looking for a tumble in the hay? Whatever he was up to last night must have whetted his appetite. What on earth's got into him? I've never seen him act this way before.'

Finally Seebohn returned to Boden and said,

'I'm hungry enough to wipe out a plate of Wurst and at least three Wiener Schnitzel. There's got to be something decent to eat.'

'Do whatever you want, Seebohn, but whatever it is, stay happy.'

Boden turned his attention to the map once more, to pick out their exact whereabouts; but he did not have the large scale section covering this area, that they should have drawn with last night's petrol, maybe because they hadn't been expected to go so far north. The Michelin was scaled two kilometres to the centimetre so that it was not over precise on the kind of detail that Boden needed. It was therefore difficult to mark a clear and practical exit from the valley in which this farm was buried.

In the background, Boden heard Seebohn smashing down the farmhouse door with the sledgehammer and then there were sounds of his rummaging about inside. Finally he emerged carrying a ham by its shank and an armful of tomatoes.

'There's no bread,' he called out, 'but I'll bring a couple of bottles of wine.'

Wundshammer said,

'It's a pity there's no decent beer in these parts, it's as thin as gnat's piss and just about as potent. Still, if that's the best you can do, I wouldn't say no to a mid-morning snack.'

In fact the corpulent driver was not really interested in the food, being more concerned with the progress of Richter and Haagen towards the sea. Then he said to Boden,

'Anyway, I don't get it. Why did you have to tip off Haagen about that tank?'

Boden looked up from the map.

'Don't worry about it, he won't get far. They won't even know how to change the plugs on that Anglo-Saxon number.'

Seebohn climbed onto the engine grille and said,

'You can see the sea from up here.'

'That's no surprise, it's only eight kilometres off.'

'Then what are we waiting for here?'

'I'm working out the best way of making it without being arrested by the Gestapo. Besides, there's no great hurry.'

'That's news to me.'

'Von Dressen says that the Tommies are digging their heels in at Calais and there may be hold ups before the mediums arrive. After the last few days, I'm not enthusiastic about advancing to contact. Besides, I shouldn't really be doing it at all with my arm in its present condition.'

Boden's memory flickered over the crowded moments of their battles at the Maginot Fort, with the Somua, and the action south of Arras. He found it difficult to believe it had all happened so quickly. At last he said,

'Believe me, I could use twenty four hours with my head down.'

'Couldn't we all?'

'There's no sign of that in your case, Seebohn, not after last night at any rate.'

'Don't worry, I do it all on Pervitin.'

Boden said,

'Is that right? I don't need pep pills.'

They cut off slices from the ham in silence, cramming the looted meat into their mouths with the tomatoes. Boden didn't want any wine, so Seebohn finished one bottle. Wundshammer, having taken a mouthful from the second, pulled a face.

'You can tell you're out of the wine country now and that's a fact. They'll drink anything where the vines won't grow. This tastes like bull's urine. Have the other half, Seebohn.'

'I wonder who lived here?' Seebohn asked reflectively.

'Christ knows, and anyway, who cares? Wundshammer, it's time for us to roll.'

* * *

Half an hour later they were out of the valley, climbing up the spine of a long, kidney shaped hill, the chalk overgrown with coarse grass. There was little cover to speak of apart from a few wind-blown trees. By this time, Boden was too tired to care if they were in silhouette as they traversed the hill crest, but he was not over-worried, since he no longer believed in the existence of French anti-tank guns, which seemed to have done a vanishing act together with the rest of the French Army. Everywhere he looked the hills were bare except for a few stunted hawthorns pointing permanently away from the sea wind. From time to time as they passed a flock of lambs, Seebohn would come out with a sheep imitation, roaring with laughter as they scattered before the tracks of the oncoming panzer.

'Just like the French Army. Look, there's General Weygand and the one with the moustache looks like Lord Gort and there's General Ga-aa-aa-melin.'

To their left, but well behind, Boden could make out the British Light Tank crewed by Redwitz, Loeker and Haagen. Boden guessed that they must have stopped to forage for petrol. From where they had now arrived on the rolling hills west of Cap Gris Nez, the Unteroffizier commanded a view that stretched from Boulogne to Calais.

Boden picked up his glasses. Four kilometres away Route Nationale 40 passed through the small seaside resort of Sangatte Plage. Approaching it from the north, he could make out the progress of a solitary panzer, crawling down the road in the direction of Le Touquet.

'I do believe that's Richter, the sod.'

'If it is, we've had it. We'll never make it now.'

'Don't bet on it, Richter might push his luck. Besides it doesn't look all that easy to get down to the sea where he is.'

'Big drop, is there?'

'It looks like it.'

'Good. I hope he falls over the edge and breaks his neck.'

'We better get going, then.' Boden braced himself against

the turret hatch so that he would not bang his right arm, and watched the land stretching out ahead of them, rolling away to the north as the chalk downs changed to the flat Flemish plain. Beyond, through the haze, he could make out the dim outline of the Dover cliffs, beyond the Cap Gris Nez lighthouse. 'O.K., Wundshammer, let's beat Richter to Sangatte Plage and go and buy a bucket and spade.'

As they dropped below the crest, Boden could see quite clearly that it was Richter's panzer.

'Step on it, Wundshammer, if you want to get your feet wet before he does.'

'I don't want to slip a track.'

'I don't much care if you drop a bollock, provided we make it ahead of Richter.'

Wundshammer began to drive really hard, so that the Mark 2 panzer plunged and bucketed dangerously as they followed one of the many tracks that criss-crossed the short-grassed chalk.

As the panzer half slid, half drove through a thin hawthorn hedge marking the outskirts to Sangatte Plage, Boden briefly caught sight of Richter's panzer to the north as it painfully negotiated the hairpin bends leading from the chalk downs to sea level.

Wundshammer found himself in a lane that would bring them out at the centre of Sangatte Plage. As they came to the main street that ran parallel with the beach, Wundshammer said,

'Look, washing day.'

The windows of the surrounding houses, although deserted and shuttered, were draped with white sheets, table cloths, towels and even handkerchiefs.

'They've given up,' said Seebohn. 'Given up completely. They must be only waiting for the armistice.'

'Not until we've booted out the B.E.F.,' said Boden.

As he spoke they came to the tiny Place de la République, now jammed with an abandoned British Transport Column. Some of the trucks had been driven through the sea wall railings, but in most cases there clearly had not been enough time for that. The majority stood where they had been parked, their tyres methodically slashed, engine blocks shattered and radiators smashed.

Boden told Wundshammer to halt and then glanced round the deserted Square.

Seebohn said,

'What's that?'

Littered around the 1914–18 War Memorial, with its palm sprays and bronze warrior waving his Adrian helmet in one hand and an 1886 model rifle in the other, were hundreds of scattered leaflets.

The Wireless Operator slid down the hull of the panzer to examine one. Then he shouted out,

'It's in English. Listen to this:

"You are surrounded
The match is ended
Throw down your arms
We take prisoners." '

He held one out for Boden, who turned it over to find a map of the Franco-Belgian Frontier, with blank pockets marked with a union jack at Boulogne, Calais and Dunkirk. The pockets were surrounded by swastikas.

Boden now saw why Sangatte Plage had been spared the attentions of the Luftwaffe's Bertas. Evidently the Staff had preferred to use leaflets to induce a surrender.

'Well the B.E.F. don't seem very interested, that's all I can say. I don't see them streaming out to greet us with their hands in the air.'

The Unteroffizier was now aware of the distant rumble of Richter's panzer advancing into Sangatte Plage from the north. Meanwhile, Seebohn walked excitedly towards the first of several paved passages leading to the promenade above the sea wall where access to the beach was gained by a flight of cast iron steps.

The Wireless Operator called out over his shoulder,

'Anyway, it looks like we're the first. And I'll personally make sure that no other swine can argue about that.'

* * *

Three miles out to sea from Sangatte Plage, Lieutenant

Duncan RNVR swept the resort with his glasses. Since dawn that morning he had been patrolling the western approaches to the Channel Straits in MTB 207. By now his attention was equally divided between monitoring U-Boat activity at the periphery of the supply and evacuation lanes, on which the B.E.F. totally depended. In addition, he had to observe the progress of the German Blitzkrieg along the coast.

Already that morning, patrolling the Pas de Calais at forty five knots, Duncan had reported targets on the road south from Le Touquet and called down interdictory fire from ships of the patrolling Channel Squadron to his rear.

Although the three 1000 hp Rolls Royce power Merlin engines of the seventy foot Vosper boat had an endurance of a thousand miles, cruising at 22 knots, the MTB's coxswain had had to advance the throttles more than once that day to avoid Heinkels, and MTB 207 was already on the reserve tanks. For this reason Lieutenant Duncan was about to make a course back to Folkstone when he hesitated.

'Should there be anyone in Sangatte Plage, Coxswain?'

'No, they all pulled out last night.'

'Seems as though there's a straggler.'

Through his glasses, Duncan observed the progress of a solitary Mark VIA Light Tank hurrying northwards obviously to Calais.

'He's going to be in trouble, if he's not very careful.'

The Coxswain said gloomily,

'I thought we'd used up all our tanks at Arras.'

'I'm moving inshore to take a closer look. Reduce speed to ten knots as we approach.'

'Reduce speed to ten knots as we approach. Aye, aye, sir.'

The Coxswain moved back the throttle by touch, being able to gauge the exact speed by the sound of the engines.

Examining the sea front once more, Lieutenant Duncan could make out the silhouette of the British tank quite distinctly as it entered Sangatte Plage. Now he focused on the Square, surrounded by a cluster of buildings, and sucked in his breath as he marked the grey hull of a German panzer.

There was a second AFV half in and out of a sidestreet.

Lieutenant Duncan said between his teeth,

'The way he's going he's certain to hit trouble.'

The RNVR Lieutenant reflected a moment, and decided that the situation was much too confused to call down a barrage from HMS Atherstone, Intrepid and Afghan who were screening the Channel seven miles behind with just such targets in mind.

He did not have to look at the chart to know that the tide was still flowing so that with MTB 207's two foot six inch draught they would be able to run in right up to the beach.

'Pass the word to the gunners – static target, German Armour at town centre. Fire at will. Own troops' Mark VIA Light Tank entering town along south coast road.'

* * *

Seebohn moved down the passageway to the beach, passing the shuttered shop fronts that concealed chocolate, parasols, beach balls, toy boats and postcards, filled with the blind urge to be first to the sea. It was quite ridiculous to feel so strongly about something so relatively unimportant as a week's leave in Paris. It was the kind of feeling he should have had the moment he had decided to risk his life and win the Iron Cross.

Although he held his machine pistol at the ready it was an empty gesture, since he had omitted to clip in a magazine. He was at that time totally vulnerable, disarmed by the implicit message of the leaflets and the wrecked British trucks.

Deserted Sangatte Plage brought back memories of similar little Baltic coastal towns, empty and silent on a Sunday morning.

His mind filled with these thoughts, and emotion blocking his throat in anticipation of the triumph ahead, Seebohn failed to observe the slim, predatory silhouette of the Royal Navy motor torpedo boat, as it slid silently in through the shallow water towards the beach.

As he came to the sea wall, all Seebohn could think of was reaching the sea, breaking and ebbing thirty yards away across the smooth white sand.

He did not see the boat until he had taken another ten

steps forward, but by then it was already too late, as the sea ahead exploded in a blaze of light and the machine gunner on the rear gun platform of MTB 207 swept the area between the sea wall and the surf with .303, while the coxswain brought round the boat to bear the 20mm Oerlikon on the grey, box-like shadow standing beside the Sangatte Plage War Memorial.

The pattern of shots across Seebohn's body was uneven and irregular, due to the infinitesimal rise and fall of the MTB's gun platform in the swell, so although Seebohn initially received two tracer rounds through his left shoulder, the impact of which being enough to throw him backwards off balance a distance of two metres, four more rounds entered his stomach at an angle, ploughing up into his thorax, except for the last, which glanced up and out of his rib cage and across his chest, impacting in his lower jaw and fracturing it.

The damage suffered by Seebohn's body was in consequence final, as on their exit the tracer bullets removed a section of his lung and shoulder blade, tearing open the axillary artery in the process.

A further round passed through his spleen to lodge in the wall of his right ventricle. The last bullet to strike the wireless operator passed through the small intestine and colon before becoming embedded in his third lumbar vertebra.

Seebohn lay on his back, confused by the sound of the machine gun and the distant crack of the Oerlikon, still unable to understand what had happened to him and puzzled as to why it was suddenly impossible for him to see the sea. There was an unusual warmth at his upper left arm, which also puzzled him, since he could not turn his head to see his life blood draining away through the severed axillary artery.

Neither did he understand the pain when he tried to move. After a little he stopped trying, but when he opened his eyes he found the sky that had been so blue all that spring had now grown misty. Realising it was still morning, he began to wonder why it was growing dark so early.

* * *

As Richter's Mark VIA Light Tank turned the corner into the Rue Gambetta, Lieutenant Duncan RNVR was suddenly aware that a scarlet swastika flag was draped across the rear of the engine compartment.

He immediately took up the radio telephone, to open the wireless link that would connect him with the gunnery control officer on HMS Afghan.

* * *

Boden had seen the death of Seebohn on the beach but he was now concerned with meeting the menace of the present attack. He was also angry that it should have happened at all. Through his visor he could see the torpedo boat's long narrow outline as it started to back off the beach, while the walls of the surrounding houses still resounded and crumbled at the impact of 20mm high explosive shells fired at the rate of three a second.

Watching the shells explode, Boden realised that the MTB could have no armour piercing shot.

'Move it. Get down towards the beach, Wundshammer. We're going to get that bastard.'

When he had found the field of fire at the entrance to the passage which Seebohn had gone down, he laid the 2cm kwk 30. The first round skipped along the surface of the sea and vanished, but as the MTB turned sideways on into full profile, his second shot ploughed through the one inch timbers just above the waterline, passing through the casing of the port drive housing and fracturing the propeller shaft.

There was consequently an immediate drop in power which swung the bow of the MTB inshore. Meanwhile the red hot shot began to ignite the wooden formers underpinning the planing hull and the fire steadily increased and caught hold, aided by the steady drip of lubricating oil from the fractured shaft. The fire soon became a blaze at the moment when Boden's third shot passed at an angle through the hull, making its exit below the starboard torpedo tube, missing the warhead of the eighteen inch torpedo, lying in the starboard torpedo bay, by not more than ten centimetres.

His final shot, laid at the same angle, ploughed into the wooden hull, as the coxswain desperately fought for directional control and the crippled MTB continued to turn to port. However this time the shot struck the 500lb Torpex charge of the eighteen inch torpedo.

The resulting explosion instantly killed Lieutenant Duncan, his second officer and the crew of six at their various stations aft, ripping apart the turrets and upper and lower control positions in a sheet of flame, transforming them into disparate arcs of wreckage as the hull, engine room and decking totally disintegrated. All that was left was the burning wooden shell of the forward planing hull, which flared brightly for an instant, before it tilted forward and twisted onto its port side, and, hissing and steaming, slid forward under the sea.

Richter said over the platoon net,

'Congratulations, you'll be able to add a blue victory ring to your gun barrel.'

Boden only grunted an acknowledgement. Although he never liked Seebohn, he was still angry at his death at the close of the campaign. This was stronger than his secondary feeling of relief that now he would not have to endure his company in Paris.

'All right, Wundshammer, let's get down on the beach.'

Wundshammer crashed his way into the passage leading to the sea wall, but as he turned, the port offside trackguard tore away the soft steel shutters of the Café-du-Nord and removed part of the outside wall to reveal the floor tiles, marble and cast iron tables and the counter on which bottles of sweets and glass domed cakestands were standing.

When they reached the sea wall, Wundshammer asked,

'Where to now?'

Boden said,

'I'm not leaving any panzer man like this; come and give me a hand.'

Wundshammer climbed out through the driver's hatch and removed the shovel that was strapped to the side of the hull.

Boden then insisted that they share the digging, using his

left hand to spoon out sand, taking turns with the driver. When they got down to half a metre, Richter's panzer appeared above the sea wall, followed shortly after by the Mark VIA Infantry Tank.

Wundshammer found the whole business irritatingly slow until they hit the stratum of damp sand below the surface.

The driver spat and said,

'He certainly missed his chance to go to Paris.'

Seebohn still lay on his back where he had fallen, and both men were strangely reluctant to touch him, although, apart from the red mottling below his fractured jaw, he looked less unsightly than many of the bodies they had seen over the last few days. Seebohn's left hand was stretched out as though in feeble protest.

Boden said,

'The bastard even had to go to his grave improperly dressed. Those trousers are awful.'

Then he climbed laboriously down into the two metre hole and carefully arranged a shelter triangle at the bottom of the trench.

'All right, let's get him in.'

When they lifted Seebohn, his head lolled and his arm slumped.

Wundshammer said,

'There's enough blood. It's like a pork butcher's underneath.'

After they had slipped Seebohn into the grave Boden covered the dead Wireless Operator with a second Zeltbahn triangle.

'Goodbye, Seebohn.'

The other panzer crews were standing around the open grave, staring; it was the first time they had seen anything like this and they were all of them shocked that it had happened to someone they had known and who, not so long ago, had picked up their bills at Arras.

Wundshammer got irate when he saw them standing around gaping, and shouted at Redwitz,

'Don't just stand there waiting to take a photograph! You can see the Herr Unteroffizier's arm's all parcelled up in a bandage, and I'm buggered if I'm going to fill that lot in all by myself!'

Richter and Redwitz shuffled over to the grave and began to kick the sand in with their boots while Stossen pushed sand over the bloodstains.

When they had filled it up Wundshammer patted round the mound with his shovel.

'All right,' said Boden. 'That's enough for now. We can leave the rest to the grave salvage company, except we should mark the spot.'

'How will you do that?' Wundshammer asked, 'this beach is so perfect there's not even a bit of driftwood to use as a marker.'

Boden said,

'I know, the English tank. Redwitz, take off their aerial and bring one of their flags.'

'Right away.'

Redwitz returned a minute later, having unscrewed the two metre aerial and found a little, square, yellow signal flag.

'Has anyone got a pen or something to write with?'

Wundshammer said,

'There's bound to be something suitable in that shop I bumped into.'

'All right, but don't spend all day rifling the till.'

They waited in silence as Redwitz carefully pushed down the signal aerial at the head of the mound of heaped sand.

Wundshammer returned with a glass cake dish in each hand loaded with chocolate éclairs and a bottle of Calvados under each arm.

'For the wake,' he explained. 'Besides, we never had our dessert back there on that farm.'

Wundshammer carefully put down the Calvados and cakes and felt in his tunic pocket for the indelible pencil he had taken.

Boden lettered on the flag,

FRITZ SEEBOHN – 6 PLATOON – 31 PANZER REGIMENT.

'What's the date?'

Nobody could tell him.

'Well, let's call it May the 24th. It won't matter much if we're a couple of days out, more or less and, in that case, we may even have miraculously extended Seebohn's lifespan.'

When he had put in this date, he had still only filled up the top half of the flag.

Wundshammer said,

'Shouldn't you put in something else? A poem or something? The sort of thing you read in the "In Memoriam" columns of newspapers? "Fallen for Greater Germany" or "A hero's death against the Reich's enemies".'

Redwitz said,

'You must be joking, what you must really mean is "Here lies the biggest tin arse Nazi between here and Berlin".'

Richter said,

'That's a bit strong. But, on the other hand, I don't see how you can put on any of the guff that Wundshammer's proposing. A better compromise would be "Fallen while ensuring he won a dirty week in Paris", or "Fallen because he did not see the English machine gun in time".'

'You can't put things like that.'

'I don't give a stuff about what you can or you can't put. I can tell you I'd prefer to have it straight from the shoulder if it had been me instead of him.'

In the end, Boden simply drew a large swastika to fill up the big space and then printed in as an afterthought,

LUXEMBOURG TO THE CHANNEL – MAY 1940

By now, Wundshammer had opened one of the Calvados bottles and said,

'I'll just see whether this is worth drinking. Some of this French juice can be pretty rough.'

After he had swallowed a third of the bottle he paused to smack his lips in apparent satisfaction and said,

'Not a bad drop.'

This made Redwitz mad, and he snatched the bottle away from Wundshammer.

'What do you mean "not bad"? I don't understand your attitude, Wundshammer, it's unseemly. If this charade is supposed to be a wake, at least you should show some respect.'

Wundshammer didn't move a muscle.

'It's all right for you to sound off, you didn't have to share a turret with the bugger. But be my guest; go ahead.'

Wundshammer then stretched down to one of the glass cake stands and, removing the dome, took out two chocolate éclairs and crammed them into his mouth.

'Hmm, delicious. Here's to you, Seebohn.'

Richter and Loeker immediately followed his example but spat out their first mouthful.

'What the hell are you playing at, Wundshammer? The cream's as sour as a whore's armpit.'

At the same time Redwitz had turned red in the face as he tried to emulate the driver, for, removing the bottle from his lips, he began to cough and splutter, his eyes watering.

'What the hell is this stuff? Embalming fluid?'

Wundshammer took another chocolate éclair.

'You are fussy about your food, aren't you? That apple-jack's a local speciality. Didn't you notice all those orchards we've been driving through? They don't use the apples just to prop open the roast boar's mouth. Give me back the bottle if you don't like it and I'll cool down Seebohn, he'd appreciate it. Are you there, Seebohn? I hope you're finding it warm enough where you are, Seebohn. Here, have a nice cool drink.' He tipped the remaining half bottle of Calvados over the grave.

'Yes,' said Redwitz, 'and you can have a good tuck in to these goodies as well, Seebohn. You're about all they're fit for, if it wasn't for pigs like Wundshammer. Sorry we can't afford flowers, but there isn't a long ship to cremate you in either. Nor even your favourite Wagner record.'

Just as he was placing the two glass cake stands on the burial mound, they all dropped instinctively as they heard the deafening rumble of six express trains simultaneously passing over their heads and the first broadside of fifteen inch shells delivered by HMS 'Revenge' bracketing the sea wall, crumbling many of the façades of the over-looking houses like paper.

Boden cursed as, forgetting about his right arm, he tried to use it in his fear to scramble to his feet. Once he had managed to get up he shouted to the others, waving his left arm,

'To the north! Over there! That way!'

Running for the Mark 2 panzer he could hear Wundshammer thudding away behind him.

The second terrifying salvo arrived as Wundshammer, engaging bottom gear, began to plough through the sand towards a ramp a hundred metres away which gave access to the road, which, up to that point, ran above the sea wall.

This time the salvo exploded just above the tideline where they had been giving Seebohn his send off. Glancing back, Boden could only see a drifting cloud of sand and smoke and, high in the air above, the flicker of a yellow flag.

11 Calais

They stopped three kilometres to the south of Bleriot Plage, which was really a suburb of Calais, when the road ran down to the sea.

Boden could hear the sound of artillery to the north. Then the Unteroffizier at last remembered to switch on his headset and became instantly aware of the monotonous repetition of his call-sign. Switching to transmit, he answered the call. Leutnant Von Dressen sounded unhappy when he spoke.

'What the devil's happening, Boden? Or don't you bother to keep wireless watch any more?'

Boden said,

'We've just been burying our wireless operator, Herr Leutnant.'

Von Dressen said,

'That explains it, does it? Where are you now?'

'Where the Frenchman first flew across the Channel, somewhere a little short of Calais.'

'Good God,' said the Leutnant. 'I never thought you were up as far as that.'

'What d'you mean, Herr Leutnant?' Boden said uneasily, since he had an innate fear of being cut off.

'There's an order through to re-group. Tenth Panzer are moving in to take Calais tomorrow. If they don't get immediate results, it'll be up to the Luftwaffe then.'

'So what are we expected to do?'

'Sit tight, where you are.'

'What? And watch Calais burning?'

'If you like, you shouldn't find that too much hardship. By the way, you'd better give me the names for the Paris leave passes.'

Boden said,

'We've been too busy to think of anything like that, Herr

Leutnant. Particularly with Seebohn arranging to get killed so inconveniently.'

'Well, now you'll have a chance to do something about it. Have a competition between the crews, so it can be decided once and for all.'

'I hadn't thought of that, Herr Leutnant. I'll certainly let you know. I'll have a radio watch kept in Redwitz' panzer in case there are any new developments, such as being shelled by the British fleet.'

'What did you say, Boden?'

'I'll tell you the whole story some other time, Herr Leutnant.'

The Unteroffizier climbed out of the panzer and glanced at the smoking smudge of Calais to the north, that was due to be attacked in the morning; at least it seemed doubtful that they would have to participate. With the recent memory of Seebohn's death, he hoped they wouldn't.

Then he told Wundshammer to get the other crews while he stood staring at the sea which washed fitfully up and down against the shore one hundred metres away.

When they stood round him, Boden said,

'We can stand down for the moment, the Herr Leutnant says that nothing much will happen till tomorrow.'

Stossen asked,

'Will we get the Goulash Cannon?'

Boden said,

'Who knows? You should have hung on to those chocolate éclairs.'

Redwitz asked,

'So what happens next?'

'The Herr Leutnant wants to know which of the crews is the one that's going to relax in Paris at his expense.'

Richter said,

'I thought Seebohn had made it, so surely yours must be the lucky crew, Herr Unteroffizier.'

Boden said,

'Don't let's cloud the issue with Seebohn. Seebohn didn't make it to the sea, not technically, he was the kind of fanatic who was never destined to make it anywhere. No, don't let's worry about him, he never actually dipped his toe in the Channel and that's what was agreed. Since we're all here, except for him and Munchausen, I'm sure you understand that the Leutnant would like us to do the job properly. So, the first man from any crew that gets to the sea, as from now, wins for his crew. All right?'

Loeker said,

'That sounds fair enough.'

'Just one other detail, before I forget,' added Boden, 'I want Haagen on wireless watch in my panzer. That'll even out the crews as well.'

Redwitz was looking preoccupied as he said,

'All right, Haagen, off you toddle, you heard the Herr Unteroffizier.'

When Haagen had left, Redwitz continued,

'I'm not so sure about all this. There's something funny about those dunes.'

A single strand of barbed wire separated the road they were standing on from the way down to the beach. The wind had uncovered a round, rusty object the size of a small cooking pot, buried in the sand of the nearest dune.

'That looks like some obsolete French mine to me, but none the less dangerous for that.'

Boden smiled and said,

'Well, if you're right and it is, that'll sort out the men from the boys. You can always find a way round if you like, but some of the others might prefer the direct route and get there before you. It could be a long hike round.'

'Bloody hell,' said Richter, 'What a way to end the race.'

'Don't blame me,' Boden said, 'it hasn't exactly been healthy wherever we've landed up. First the British MTB, then shelled by warships; a French minefield should be child's play after that. It's just the way the cards have fallen.'

'But a minefield. That's quite mad. Who on earth would plant one here?'

'Who knows? Maybe the French want to keep something from us.'

'Whatever it is, I don't like it.'

'That's up to you, Richter. Like I said, you can always walk round.'

'Why don't we all do just that?'

But in spite of the tremor of unease that ran through the panzer crews, nobody moved, although it obviously disheartened them to have come up against this final, dangerous obstacle before getting to the sea.

Redwitz picked up a stone.

'Maybe it's all a spoof. Maybe we're getting worked up over nothing. Let's find out.'

At the fourth throw, Richter registered a direct hit on the rusty object, while the rest of the crews lay crouched behind their panzers. After two seconds, the dune exploded with a roar.

'Now we bloody well know,' Richter said grimly.

Then he got up and shouted to Stossen,

'Oh, to hell with it! Move your carcase and bring two cleaning rods. The ones we use to swab out the 2cm kwk 30.'

The others watched incredulously when Stossen returned and Richter moved to the edge of the wire, taking one of the metre and a half steel rods and beginning to poke the sand ahead with it delicately.

'Get on with it, Stossen, you do want to hang out your flag in the shadow of the Eiffel Tower, don't you?'

Stossen bit his lip, but began to work methodically beside Richter, edging forward in obvious distaste to help him uncover any mines that lay ahead.

Redwitz, who had been staring at the pair of them as though he was hypnotised, suddenly got up and shouted,

'Bloody hell, I'm not standing for this! Bring a couple of satchels of stick grenades, Loeker. We'll show these bastards really how to do it.'

Then he ran fifty metres down the road and, as soon as Loeker had arrived, he began to toss the grenades at regular intervals across the minefield, running from crater to crater after they had exploded and set off anything unpleasant in the immediate vicinity by repercussion. In a few minutes a cloud of sand and smoke lay along the corridor they had created.

Not to be outdone, Boden picked up his machine pistol, holding it lefthanded and clipping on a magazine, emptying half of it into the open area to the left of the dune. The ground immediately erupted in a series of explosions, and as the clouds of sand subsided, Boden and Wundshammer charged forward and dived for cover. Then, lying down, they opened up again on the ground ahead, exploding a string of mines along the width of the minefield.

Boden glanced over his shoulder, judging that he was now almost level with Redwitz. Then he saw that Redwitz had stopped, having nearly used up all the grenades.

Realising that they now had a long way to catch up, Richter and Stossen began to take bigger and bigger risks. Richter stabbed at the ground as far ahead as he could stretch and, if it seemed clear, Stossen would leap onto this patch. Using this revised and risky technique, it wasn't long before they began to make progress.

Boden clipped on a new magazine and was just about to fire when he saw that there was a concrete bunker built into the dune to his immediate right. He was considering the best course of action to take, when six French soldiers emerged from the dug out at the side, all clutching grubby handkerchiefs in their raised right hands. Boden could see that their leader, a Corporal, had neglected the razor for several days and that a cigarette hung wetly out of the corner of his mouth. The rest of his appearance was equally unmilitary, since his ill-fitting greatcoat swept the ground. Boden now realised that as he had swung round towards the French, he had covered them automatically with his machine pistol.

'Don't shoot, comrades, don't shoot. We've had enough after that bombardment.'

'Then just stay where you are.'

'Don't worry, sirs, we're not armed. This is an observer's post to watch the Channel shipping and give advance warning of air raids.'

But Boden had already lost interest.

'Piss off,' he shouted, now that he saw that Richter, totally unconcerned at this new development, was now not more than ten metres from the tide line.

'No sir, we are not armed. We are garrison troops. We wish to surrender our strongpoint.'

To Boden the Corporal looked more like a middle aged tramp than anything else with his half smoked 'Troupe' cigarette, his dirty hands and face and his unpolished brass greatcoat buttons and Adrian Helmet Badge. Turning his back on the prisoners, the Unteroffizier saw that since Redwitz and Stossen were out of grenades, they were now crawling forward on their stomachs, seeking out mines by touch.

Boden swung the machine pistol into his hip, once again blasting the ground ahead, and then, as he came to the hard sand above the tideline, he did not care any more, charging ahead through the safety of the high water mark and collapsing face down in the surf.

A few minutes later the rest of them were through and ran over to him as Richter called out,

'That's fair enough! You made it, you lucky sod. You made it!'

Boden smiled.

'Don't worry,' he said getting to his feet. 'I'll see what can be arranged in the way of leave. After what you've done, I reckon the Leutnant owes all of you a favour.'

He pulled a bloodstained paybook out of his tunic pocket.

'You might even win a consolation prize. I feel sure that Seebohn would like you to have a share of his petty cash. As we all know, he carried a heavy roll, although he never had much occasion to use it.'

Suddenly Boden was aware of the aroma of stale garlic combined with 'Troupe' cigarettes and turned to find the French Corporal standing apologetically at his elbow, still clutching his handkerchief. Clearing his throat he looked fearfully up at Boden.

'I must tell you, sir, there is an easier way across the minefields that our sentries sometimes use when they are called out. It is safer and quicker. If you follow me, I will take you and your friends back.'

Boden looked at Wundshammer incredulously and rested his good arm across his shoulder.

They still had not stopped laughing by the time the Frenchman had led the way back to their panzers.